TRIGGER WARNING:

This novel contains strong language. This novel contains mental illness and manipulation. This novel contains violent situations. Killings take place that are described in detail. Please read with discretion.

TABLE OF CONTENTS

CHAPTER ONE

"This is going to be good for us," I say, smiling confidently after my words. I glance over at my light-skinned husband, noticing him sporting an unsure face, "Ray, I'm serious."

He nods his head hesitantly, "I hope you're right."

I reposition my body, staring at the paved road in front us. My husband has been driving down the interstate for hours; hands 10 and two, cruise control set at the speed limit of 70 MPH, making sure not to cut anyone off or intimidate other drivers.

Safe and by the book.

Ever since he got out of the psych ward a few months ago, he's been walking as straight and narrow as humanly possible. I guess I understand where he's coming from since his past was so horrendous, but still…

You have to live a little.

"You hungry?" He asks, staring straight ahead with his words. He refuses to take his eyes off the road for a second. I hump my shoulders, even though he can't see me doing it.

"I don't know. You?" He humps his shoulders as well.

"I mean, I can eat. I'm on the fence about it. I wanted to use you as the deciding factor." He smiles and makes eye contact with me for the first time in hours. I blush once his hazel eyes meet mine.

"Aren't we almost there?" He nods his head yes.

"We are, but don't forget, the movers will be arriving right after us, and we still have yet to grocery shop for our new place." I nod at the realization.

"You're right, we don't have food there." I make a pondering face, "Ok, then. Restaurant food it is." I smile after my statement, but he looks uneasy. I rub his back gently.

"Everything is going to be fine. No one knows us here. That's why we picked this place, remember?" He gestures that he does. He takes a deep breath.

"Yeah... I guess you're right. Everything will be fine." I lean over to kiss him on the cheek.

"That's the spirit. So, where should we stop?"

***

"Two, please," I say to the hostess once we approach the small podium after walking inside of a local eatery. She smiles before grabbing two menus and walking us down the aisle.

"Table or booth?" She asks once we make it near a set of empty tables. I glance at my husband, whose face is so pale with nervousness that I decide to make the decision solo.

"Booth," I answer quickly. She sits the menus on the table after he and I slide inside.

"Your waitress will be with y'all shortly," she informs us with a strong southern drawl. My husband and I give her a quick grin before she scurries away.

"See! So far, so good," I say in a positive tone. I reach over the table to grab my husband's hand. I squeeze it lovingly, prompting him to do the same. He works hard to swallow his swiftly developing anxiety. He concentrates on his breaths just like his therapist showed him. After a minute or two, he finally calms down. I wink at him, which is my subtle way of letting him know that I'm proud of him. We release each other's hands to study our menus.

"Hmm, the fish looks good," I utter without taking my eyes off the picture of the delicious looking meal. I read the description before finally looking up at my husband's face, "What do you think?"

"You're right, it does look good, but we just had fish yesterday, so I really don't have a taste for that." I glance back down at the menu.

"So, what do you have a taste for, then?" He doesn't respond right away, turning the page of the menu to look over more options.

"What about the steak? It's been a while since we've had a big, juicy ribeye. I love that cut of meat. You know, the farmers take a nice, sharp knife and go against the cow's ribs to get it..." I get terrified while listening to his words. My heart rate speeds up rapidly, and I cover my face from his view with the menu. I close my eyes tightly, trying my best to stop the horrible images from flashing in my head. Blood and flesh are all I see, along with the words:

He slaughtered them like cattle.

"Hey, baby, you ok?" I fix my expression the best I can before lowering the menu to look at him. I smile as authentically as possible before nodding my head yes. He stares at me worriedly, "You sure?"

"Yes, babe," I answer immediately. "You're right, the steak does sound good. Let's get that." I quickly bring an end to the subject. He stares at me a little longer before looking at his menu again.

"Ok. I bet it's going to be to die for."

CHAPTER TWO

"That's fine. You can leave it there," I tell the mover after he brings in the last box. Just as tired as I am of seeing him, I'm sure he feels the exact same way about me. He leaves out the front door without saying a word. I close it as soon as he crosses the threshold.

"Is that it?" Ray asks after coming around the living room corner.

"Yes, thank God," I answer, walking over and sitting on the couch where the mover sat anywhere. My husband joins me.

"Good, because I was hoping we could get a little alone time." He leans over and sticks his face in my neck. I giggle as his kisses tickle me.

"You want to get frisky when we don't even have a sheet on the bed yet?"

"Bed? Who said anything about a bed? I'm about to take you right here on this couch!" He forces me back and pounces on me like a wild animal. I laugh hysterically after he starts tickling my sides. He nibbles on my neck, causing me to cringe up from the overwhelming feeling. He pauses to stare into my eyes.

"Brit, you know how much I love you, right?" I nod my head yes without saying a word. His face gets serious, "I know it was hard to leave everyone and everything we've ever known behind like we did, but it was just so damn-" I place my hand over his mouth to shush him. I smile gently.

"You don't have to say it, babe, I already know. And leaving was a little bittersweet, but it was time to move on, anyway. We were outgrowing that place." He nods his head in agreement before slowly moving his lips towards mine. He plants a big wet one on me, causing my toes to curl in my Nike running shoes. I lean back until my head rests on the couch pillow. I submit my body to him, and as usual, he does not disappoint.

***

I jump out of my sleep at the same time every night, and this night is no different. I glance at the alarm clock next to our bed and sigh after reading the time: *3:13am.*
I look over at my husband. I'm glad I didn't wake him up this time with my recurring nightmare. I thought moving would help with that…

I guess I was wrong.

I ease out of the bed, trying my best not to kick randomly scattered boxes in the dark. I maneuver quietly through our bedroom until I make it out safely. I head straight for the bathroom to relieve myself, and then to the kitchen. I want a drink of water but realize quickly that we never unpacked any glasses. I sigh and grab a bowl.

This'll have to do.

I walk into the living room toting the bowl of water, taking in my new surroundings in detail. I love the old school look of our new place. Ray isn't too crazy about the wallpapered walls, but I think it's dope. With a little touching up, this home will be perfect. Perfect to start a family, and hopefully, perfect to start over.

I stare out of the window at the full moon in the sky. Our block is so quiet, it's almost creepy. No streetlights or house lights, just people sleeping peacefully in their beds behind unlocked doors. I think about how unsafe that sounds.

You must lock your door. You have no idea what terrible things people can bring to your doorstep.

My thoughts take me back to the nightmare I had that broke my slumber. I close my eyes once the screaming in my head starts.

All those people...
All that blood...
How could he do something like that-

"Baby, you ok? What are you doing up?" I turn around suddenly when I hear Ray's voice. He stands there wearing only boxers and a confused look on his face. I sip from the bowl.

"Yeah, I just needed some water." He grins before walking over to me. His hands rest around my waist.

"I couldn't help but to notice the time. Still having those bad dreams?" I confirm his assumptions with a head nod. He looks at me worriedly.

"Brit, this has been going on for a while now. It's getting serious." I don't know what to say, so I choose to say nothing. He sighs before continuing, "You don't want to tell me what they're about and I respect that, but baby, you need to tell somebody. I keep telling you, my therapist is really good with things like this. She's-"

I walk away from him before he gets into yet another long spiel about why therapy is important, how much it's been helping him, how great his therapist is, blah,

blah, blah. In all honesty, he's the one that needs therapy, not me.

I've never killed anyone.

"That's good, dear, but I really don't think I need therapy." He looks disappointed. I ignore his facial expression.

"So, what are you going to do, then? Keep having these nightmares until they drive you crazy?" I place the bowl in the empty sink before turning around to acknowledge him.

"No. They'll stop on their own. We just moved into a healthier environment. I'm sure they'll go away; I just have to give it time."

CHAPTER THREE

My husband is in the basement when I get done unloading the last box for the kitchen. I stare out of the window, noticing how great the sunshine looks coming down from a cloudless sky. I throw on my shoes before opening the basement door to yell down the steps.

"Ray, I'm going for a walk!" I hear tools moving around before he responds.

"Ok, baby! Be careful, would ya!"

I head towards the side door to let myself out. I walk out, opting to leave the door unlocked since I plan on being gone for about 15 minutes or so.

I move steadily down our quiet block. The houses on the street are massive compared to the small Atlanta apartment we lived in prior to moving here. Once I found out that we could get a house three times the size of our apartment for the same price in Alabama, I jumped on the idea. Now, we're staying in the middle of nowhere in a town the size of my pinkie nail…

Just like we wanted it.

I walk past a brick house with a young, brown-skinned woman watering the grass. She throws her hand up in greeting as soon as she spots me strolling past her property. I speak back, smiling genuinely at her kind nature.

We didn't see much of that in Atlanta, either.

I turn the corner once I reach it. I'm surprised to see factory buildings instead of houses on the next block. I pause, wondering if I should go back the way I came or continue walking down the industrial lane.

"Fuck it," I decide, walking down the suspicious looking street. The huge buildings are eerily quiet, lingering with an almost abandoned silence. I look at my smart watch for the day and time:

Tuesday, 12:23pm.
Maybe everyone's gone to lunch.

I walk cautiously past each rusted structure. I stare into the depths of their open dark corridors, trying to piece together in my mind what each plant produces. No matter how hard I try, I can't find names or addresses on the buildings. I swallow hard at their secrecy. It's either that, or these places were permanently closed long ago.

The last building before the corner near my home is by far the spookiest. It looks as if the wind is two gusts away from blowing it down completely. I hesitate when I hear a loud, creaking noise coming from within its walls. I want to pick up my pace, but my eyes are too glued to its doorless entrance for me to move quicker. I don't blink at all while staring towards the darkness.

I'm directly in front of the building when I spot a figure approaching the doorway from the inside. I freeze in terror once one black boot comes into view, and then two. A person dressed in all black eventually emerges, sending terrifying shivers down my spine. My instincts finally kick in with my adrenaline not too far behind. My feet start moving swiftly around the corner without me having to tell them to do so. I sprint like I'm going for the gold, spotting my house a few seconds later. I rush to the side door but start to panic once I notice it's locked. I beat at the door like my life depends on it.

"Whoa! Brit, what's going on?" I rush inside and slam the door after Ray opens it. I stare out the window nervously.

"I just saw someone!" I shout hysterically. I finally turn to look at my husband's confused face.

"OK… but you went on a walk around the neighborhood, so I'm sure you saw a lot of people-"

"No! I'm telling you! I saw someone strange! They were dressed in all black and coming out of an abandoned building like some shit you'd see in a horror movie!"

"Newsflash baby, but people can wear all black. Look at me, I have on all black right now. Hell, so do you." I glance at his and my attire and realize he's right. I take a deep breath, "And you're acting as if something happened. Did this person say something to you?"
I shake my head no, "Chase you?" I shake my head again, "Ok, then, so what's the cause for alarm, again?" He walks up to me and places his hands on my waist. I look away from him embarrassingly.

"I guess there is no alarm." I think about me pounding on the door like a drama queen and I cover my face in shame. Then, I remember that I never locked the door when I left.

I should have never been pounding on the door in the first place!

I look in Ray's eyes, "Why did you lock me out?"
"What?"
"You locked me out! Why did you do that?"
"Baby, I didn't lock you out. I never touched the door-"
"Ray, I'm telling you, when I left out of here, I made sure the door was unlocked so that I could get back

in!" His baffled expression grows more serious every second.

"I was in the basement the whole time you were away. The first time I came up here was to let you in after hearing you beating like that. I thought something was wrong." I stare deep into his eyes, realizing that he's telling the truth. I put my hands on my head while feeling puzzled.

I could've sworn I left the door unlocked.

"Baby, I swear, I didn't lock the door on you. That's so cruel and unusual. Why would I do that?" I ponder for a minute, humping my shoulders after coming up with nothing.

Ray is right, he'd never do anything like that.

I sigh loudly, "Well, I guess I was wrong. Maybe I did lock the door." He grins before kissing me on the forehead.

"It's ok, baby. It happens."

CHAPTER FOUR

"No! What are you doing? Please don't! Please! No! NOOO!"

I scream out of my sleep just as the blade slices the poor victim's neck. Tears hurry down my cheeks before I grab my throat as if it was the one being slit. I breathe heavily, realizing that it was just another awful dream…

An awful dream about my husband murdering an innocent woman.

I glance over to his spot in the bed, looking confused once I notice he's not laying there. My eyes hurry towards our clock on the wooden nightstand:

1:30am.

"That's weird," I think. I swing my legs out of the bed, *"My nightmares usually don't wake me up until after 3am. Plus, my husband is usually in bed by now."* I slide on my fuzzy slippers and head towards the room door. After stepping into the hallway, I pause to listen for any type of noise.

Nothing.

I move curiously until I reach the other end of the hallway. I stare in the dark living room, and then towards the empty kitchen. I listen hard again, realizing that I can faintly hear my husband's voice. I follow it to the entrance of the basement.

"No, that's completely unacceptable. I can't do that," he whispers. It's apparent he's on the phone with someone. I glance back confusedly at the time on the stove, wondering who he'd be chatting with this time of night.

"Look, just give me more time. Everything is fine. I'm going to be fine; I promise." My curiosity gets the best of me, prompting me to ease quietly down the basement stairs. His back is facing me when I reach the bottom. I look around the dimly lit room slowly, realizing that this is my first time coming down here. He sighs loudly before glancing at his phone and ending the call. He takes steps towards a single black door directly in front of him, still unaware of me standing behind him. He reaches for a key in his pocket.

"Babe, what's going on?" Ray jumps so hard that the key falls to the floor. He spins around quickly to face me as I walk over to pick it up, "Does this key unlock that room?" He snatches it out of my hand quickly.

"Yeah, it does." I gawk at him weirdly.

"Ok… so, why is it locked?" Ray looks lost as if he's trying to conjure up an answer. He takes a step towards me.

"No reason, really. I just have all my work stuff in there." I fold my arms offendedly.

"So what. You've never locked your work equipment up before." He wraps his arms around me while smiling at me warmly.

"Baby, don't be like that. What are you doing out of bed, anyway?" The fragrance of his aftershave enters my nose, calming me down immediately. He moves in slowly to peck me on the lips.

"You know why." He glances at his phone in his hand.

"Nightmares before the witching hour? That's unlike you." I giggle at his facetiousness. He kisses my brow. I stare at his phone, instantly remembering him being on it a short time ago.

Who the hell was he talking to?

"And phone conversations this time of the night are unlike you as well." A busted expression appears on his face.

"I know, but that was my therapist. She was just checking on me."

"Your therapist? Checking on you after one in the morning? Ha!" I chuckle obnoxiously with disbelief. He places his phone in my hand.

"If you don't believe me, then look for yourself." I hesitate, staring into his serious eyes. He takes a step back and folds his arms. I swipe up on his lock screen, staring at a picture of him and I cuddling as his wallpaper. I go to his call log and immediately see the last call received:

Dr. Monroe.

I swallow my growing embarrassment as I look up in his eyes. He grins and steps back in my personal space.

"You know how important therapy is to me. Having 24-hour care is a must. There is no such thing as too late or too early when it comes to Dr. Monroe. My mental health trumps all of that." I nod my head in agreement, winking at him right after. He smiles as if he's proud of himself as well. We embrace tightly before allowing our tongues to explore each other's mouths. The atmosphere gets incredibly thick with lust.

"Why don't you let me take you upstairs and put you to bed the proper way?" He grins sexily, followed by him seductively biting his bottom lip. My heart beats wildly with anticipation. He walks towards the stairs with my hand in his.

"There will be no waking up at 3am tonight for you. I'm about to wear that ass out, I guarantee that."

CHAPTER FIVE

I'm washing the remainder of the dishes from breakfast when I hear a knock at the front door. It startles me somewhat, mainly because we have yet to get acquainted with anyone that lives in this town. I dry my hands on my apron before heading over to the door. I stare out of the peephole, opening it up after recognizing the face on the other side.

"Good morning! My name is Liz. I'm sorry if I'm bothering you, but I just wanted to come over and officially welcome you to the neighborhood." The young woman watering her grass yesterday stands in front of me talking with a strong, southern accent. I stare at her closely, realizing she's not as young as I once thought. She hands me a homemade chocolate cake right after her introduction. I thank her after the dessert goes from her hands to mine. I stare at it with an impressed look in my eyes.

"I'm sorry, I guess I should've asked you if you eat that type of stuff first." She giggles nervously and I smile. I step to the side.

"I'm not a big sugar eater, but my husband would love this. Please, come in." She slowly steps inside my home, allowing her eyes to take in the space quickly. I watch her moving around, "I'm Britney, by the way. It's nice to meet you." Her eyes finally land on me again.

"It's nice to meet you as well." We stare at each other awkwardly. I decide to carry the cake over to our small dining room table. She moves in that direction as well.

"You said you live here with your husband?" She asks, clearly trying to make small talk to get rid of the weirdness between us. I turn around to face her.

"Yes, his name is Ray. He's in the basement working right now."

"Oh?"

"Yeah. He's a graphic designer. It looks fun, but half of the time, I have no idea what he's talking about. I'm stupid when it comes to technology." I giggle awkwardly, prompting her to follow suit.

"Oh, don't be so hard on yourself. I'm sure you're great at your job." She stares at me as if her statement was an unofficial question. I hesitate.

"Uhm, well actually, I'm a stay-at-home wife."

"I admire that. People definitely underestimate how hard it is to keep a household together while raising a family." I nod my head as if I agree. "So, do you have any kids?"

"Not yet. Ray and I have only been married for six months. We were hoping to start a family here in Vella, though."

"So, that means you guys are newlyweds! Congratulations!" I smile with a quick thanks before she continues, "Yeah, Vella is nice. It's a little small, though. When I graduated, it was only 27 of us that walked across the stage." I make a shocked face and she giggles at my reaction.

"This place is tiny. The only good thing about living in such a small place is the comfort of knowing you're always safe. Nothing bad ever happens here. The last time we had something similar to a break-in was Mr. Rogers walking inside of someone else's house while he was drunk and passing out on their couch. And the last time we had a murder, well-"

"Hey, baby. I thought I heard you talking to someone up here." Ray emerges from the basement, startling us both away from our topic of conversation. He walks over and puts his arm around my waist, "Who is this?"

"Babe, this is our neighbor, Liz." Liz smiles at Ray while throwing her hand up to wave. He greets her with a head nod but doesn't say a word. "She was just welcoming us to the neighborhood. Look Ray, she even baked us a cake." I point to it on the table, but Ray barely looks at it. He makes an unpleasant face, causing me to elbow him subtly in his side. Liz notices his unwelcoming nature and eases backwards towards the door.

"It was nice meeting you both, but unfortunately, I must head to work. Britney, maybe we can chat sometime. I can fill you in on all the town gossip." I giggle while I walk with her to the exit to see her out. I turn around to look at Ray after the door closes.

"Wow. What was that all about?" He ignores my question. Instead, he heads over to the kitchen drawer to grab a knife…

His weapon of choice.

I freeze after seeing him holding the huge blade. He walks towards me with it but stops once he reaches the cake. I let out a sigh of relief.

"What was what about?" He finally responds to my question. I watch him slicing the cake, prompting me to head towards the cabinet to retrieve a couple of plates. I sit them on the table next to him.

"You acting all antisocial? You were being rude." He takes a deep breath before lifting a piece of the moist dessert and placing it on one of the plates. "Small piece, please," I say quickly before he cuts the second slice. He obliges, and then places that one carefully on the other plate as well.

"Believe me, it's not an act. I am antisocial."

"No, you're not-"

"With strangers, I am." He cuts me off quickly, using a serious tone that I hardly hear him use. I decide to leave it alone.

"Ok, baby. I'm not trying to start an argument. I was just saying." I grab two forks for us to eat with. We both place a piece of cake in our mouths at the same time, making pleasantly surprised faces right afterward. He looks at me after he finishes chewing.

"And I wasn't trying to be rude. I'm just leery about meeting new people, and you know why. What if she recognizes us?"

"She won't," I reply immediately. I place my hand on his, "We're safe here. No one will ever recognize our faces, and no one will ever find out what you did."

CHAPTER SIX

I lay in our king-sized bed, staring at a show that I'm barely watching. I want to cuddle up with my husband tonight, but it seems like ever since we've moved here, all he's been wanting to do is work. I glance at the clock on the nightstand:

11:11pm.
I guess it's going to be another night of me falling asleep by myself.

I reach for the lamp sitting next to the clock and turn it off. I leave the TV on, hoping that the noise will somehow influence my dreams.

I'm getting sick and tired of all the nightmares.

I don't know I'm asleep until I wake up. I'm still in the same position with my body facing the nightstand. My eyes go straight to the time:

2:27am.

I roll my body over to look for Ray.

His spot is still empty... I'm getting tired of this shit!

I get up quickly with an attitude.
"This is going to have to stop," I mumble to myself, sliding on my house shoes and walking out of the bedroom.

I go straight for the basement door and proceed down the stairs. I stop at the bottom with a look of confusion once I don't see Ray sitting at his desk. His computer monitor is lit up like it was recently used, but he's nowhere in sight. I move closer to read what's displayed on it:

"Local man, age 27, accused of brutally slaying a group of friends at a house party"

Tears surface in my eyes when I spot Ray's picture in black and white on the front of the newspaper article. My eyes skim over the words underneath:

"One of the victims, Amanda Laneer, was a close friend of the suspect. Authorities say he broke into her home and slaughtered her and her party guests like cattle…"

The faint sound of a woman whimpering startles me away from my reading. I jump before turning my body in the direction of the noise. I stare at the big, black door that my husband keeps locked at all times, swallowing hard after figuring out the whining is coming from inside. I tiptoe towards it, listening to the woman's sounds get louder as I get closer. I stop once I reach the door, placing my ear against it to hear better.

There's definitely someone in there!

"Hello!" I shout, twisting the locked doorknob at the same time. I hear an unknown ruffling sound, followed by loud sobbing right afterward.

"Please! Please, help me!" The woman screams frantically, causing my heart to beat out of my chest. I glance around the basement desperately in search of something to pry the door open with.

"Please, get me out of here! He- He locked me in!" Hot tears burn down my cheeks as her words singe me deeply.

I thought Ray was through with this! He promised me he was a changed man when I met him! He said he'd never hurt anyone again...

"Brit? Britney? Britney, baby... wake up." I jump out of my sleep with Ray's eyes being the first things I see. He stares at me worriedly with his hand on my shoulder. I pull away from him quickly. He looks offended.

"Brit, what's wrong? You were talking in your sleep again. It sounded like you were having another bad dream." I sit up and turn my back to him quickly. I wipe the flowing tears from my eyes. I take a deep breath before answering him.

"I'm fine," I lie, standing up right after my words. I head to the bathroom quickly and close the door. I stare at my distraught face in the mirror. I turn on the faucet and rinse the tear streaks from my face. I try to convince myself that it was just a dream, but if dreams were meant to be taken so lightly, then why do I keep having the same one over and over?

It's almost like I'm being warned.

"Ray is better now. He would never do anything to hurt anyone else," I whisper to myself. I pat my face dry with the towel next to the sink. I sigh loudly before opening the bathroom door. Ray is standing right outside of it as if he were waiting for me to come out. His shirtless body looks heavenly under the low light. He walks up to me and grabs my hand.

"I hate seeing you go through this. I wish I could help you," he says sweetly. I give his kind words a half smile.

"Falling asleep alone has been really hard on me. I need you next to me to sleep comfortably, honey." He grabs my hips after pressing his body against mine. I stare at his sandy brown chest before staring up in his eyes. He gawks at me lovingly.

"I'm sorry, baby. With all the packing and moving, I sort of fell behind at work. I'm still trying to play catch-up, but I promise Brit, I won't let you go to sleep at night anymore without me being there to hold you."

CHAPTER SEVEN

I'm bored.

For the past few days, Ray has kept his word and started going to bed with me every single night, but any time before 8pm, he's down in the basement working. He's never worked this much before.

I wonder if that's really what he's doing?

I can't believe how lonely I've been feeling lately. I never thought I'd be dealing with these emotions again. When Ray and I first got married, he was still in the asylum. I met him there a year prior when I used to volunteer in its hospice wing. I sat with the dying patients, providing them with some form of companionship in their last days. Most of their families had abandoned them. In some instances, I was the last face they saw before they passed on. I wanted them to have peace.

If not in this life, then hopefully in the next.

I was walking down the hallway one afternoon when I spotted Ray sitting at a table alone in the recreational room. I hesitated when his eyes met mine, mainly because he was the most handsome man I've ever seen before. His face was so familiar to me, like he was the man of my dreams or something. At that moment, I didn't know how, or even why really, but he had to be mine.

After subtly asking around about him, I found out the details of his horrible past:

"He killed his girlfriend and her friends," one nurse blurted out to me. A horrified expression painted across my face. She smiled at me amusingly, "But he seems to be deeply remorseful for what he did. He seems to be a normal guy. And, I'm not going to lie, that man is gorgeous. Don't know why he would want to kill his girlfriend when he could've easily had someone else."

Her words terrified me, and for a month straight, I walked past the recreational room where he'd sit every day and tried to ignore him. The truth was, I could've easily walked a different way like I did before I made a mistake and stumbled across him, but I still secretly wanted to see his face.

After all, he was the man of my dreams.

"Excuse me, miss." I stopped in my tracks. I closed my eyes tightly after realizing that *he* was actually speaking to me. My heart rate sped up before I turned around to face him.

"I've been seeing you walk past this room almost every day, and I told myself that I'm not going to let you walk past me again without me formally introducing myself to you." A wide smile appeared across my face. He took a step closer to me.

"I can tell by the way you're dressed that you're not a nurse. Are you here visiting family?" I shook my head shyly.

"No, I'm a volunteer here. I visit with the sick and elderly." An impressed smile appeared from behind his pink, juicy lips.

"Wow, that's so kind of you. You know, I could tell you were a kind person just by looking in your eyes." He flirted with me heavily and I secretly thanked the universe for sending the man I've been daydreaming about to talk to me. Reality simultaneously punched me in the gut once I spotted the nurse that told me all about his past.

He murdered the last woman he was in a relationship with!

I took a step away from him.

"Sorry, it was nice talking to you, but I have to go." I turned around quickly to hurry away from our conversation. I heard him yelling at my back.

"My name is Ray, by the way!"

"Ray?" I thought with a loving exhale.

"Ray is going to be my husband."

***

Even though I tried to go against my urges, I couldn't stay away from him. It was almost like we were meant to be, like our paths had crossed for a reason. He expressed every chance he got that he felt the same way about me, and shortly after that, the mentioning of marriage fell from his lips. *"I knew it!"* I thought, as soon as I heard that word leave his mouth, *"I knew he and I would be together forever!"*

Of course, before I could confidently entertain the thought of marrying him, we needed to talk about the terrible events that landed him in the hospital in the first place. I reluctantly asked him the dreaded question:

"So, why are you in here, anyway?" He stared at me from across the table with embarrassed eyes. He broke our eye contact before he answered.

"I know you've already heard a bunch of different stories about what I've done." He hung his head in shame. I reached for his hand from across the table.

"I want to hear it from you." He took a deep breath before looking at my hand and grabbing it.

"I blacked out one night and then woke up in a cell covered in blood. According to the police, I killed a bunch of my friends." I swallowed hard after his words. I tried to act like they didn't bother me, but I think my facial expression told him they did.

"It's ok, I'd be taken aback if someone told me that, too." He laughed nervously.

"When you say, 'blacked out', you mean you don't remember doing it?"

"I didn't at first. I didn't remember anything about that night. After the extensive therapy and even the hypnosis they put me under, I slowly started to remember things as pieces. Once I was able to put the pieces together, I was sick to my stomach for a week. I couldn't believe I was capable of doing something like that, and when they showed me the pictures of the crime scene..." He snatched his hand away and covered his mouth. He took a few more deep breaths, "They still make me want to vomit." I looked at him with a worried expression.

"So, how do you know that this 'black out' thing won't happen again?" He made strong eye contact with me for the first time since we started this difficult conversation.

"I've been working very hard to keep my emotions and mental health in check. I'm planning on receiving therapy every day for as long as I'm on this earth. If they let me out of here, I'm determined to live an ordinary life. I don't want to hurt anyone ever again, and I will especially never hurt you."

CHAPTER EIGHT

I sit around as long as I'm comfortably able to, but I'm starting to get antsy. I stare at the clock on my nightstand.

Another day is nearing its end without me doing shit.

The anger slowly rises in my chest. I'm tired of feeling this way.

"I moved away from everyone and everything I've ever known to start over with a man that I hardly ever get to spend time with anymore," I mumble out loud in an irritated voice.

"I gotta get out of here."

I throw on some comfortable leggings and an athletic tank. I put on my shoes next, opting to grab my keys this time just in case there's another issue involving mistakenly locked doors. I walk out of the house without even telling Ray I'm leaving.

It's not like he's going to notice I'm gone, anyway.

I walk down the street just like I did the last time. The sun is about to set, but the evening sky looks gorgeous. I glance around for new faces, but I have yet to see movement in most of these homes. Outside of Liz, I have no idea if people live on this block. The cars never seem to move and there's never any children outside playing. The houses don't look abandoned…

But looks can be deceiving.

I approach Liz's place, slowing down once I'm standing directly in front of it. I notice her car in the driveway and have half the mind to knock at her door. I hesitate at the thought, but at the last minute, decide to keep it moving. After all, Ray wasn't the warmest person towards her the last time we spoke. He might have ruined any chance of her and I becoming friends.

I hit the corner, but then stop in my tracks once the industrial lane comes into view. I stare down the long street of old, creaky buildings and take a step back. Fear creeps up my spine. The buildings are god-awful in the daytime but even more terrifying at night. The person I saw dressed in all black flashes across my mind, causing me to turn around completely.

Fuck that, I'm not going that way!

I stand on the corner and look around at all the different ways I can go. I want to explore further but figure it's a little too late to be covering new territory. After all, who's to say I won't stumble across another block of spooky buildings?

I walk back the way I came, ending up back in front of Liz's place.

"Fuck it," I say to myself before walking towards her porch. I ring her doorbell after climbing the steps. "I'm sorry, I hope it's not too late," I exclaim as soon as she opens the door. She smiles at me warmly.

"No, not at all. Actually, I was just about to pour myself a glass of wine and curl up with a book. Come on in, you can have a drink with me." She steps to the side eagerly as if she's glad to have company. I step inside of her modest home.

"This place is lovely," I say while looking around. Her house is small but it's cozy and elegant. Soft beige and white dominate the rooms' color schemes. Everything is so clean and neat, it's almost hard to believe that anyone lives here at all.

"You can have a seat on the couch, and I'll grab you a glass." I walk over to the fluffy sofa and sit down slowly. I spot a novel on the table that is all white, matching her decor perfectly. I pick it up to get a closer look at it.

"Pure, by Ruby Wright," I read out loud. Liz sits my glass on the living room table before joining me on the couch.

"Oh yes, I love that book. It's very hot and steamy. It helps me get through my lonely nights, that's for sure." She giggles and I do, too. She picks up the bottle of red wine and pours us both a glass. I thank her after she hands me mine.

"Lonely nights? You're not married?" She shakes her head no after taking a sip of her wine.

"We're separated." She tries to cover up a pained expression with a fake smile. I decide to leave the subject alone.

"I'm sorry about the way my husband treated you the other day. He acts like that around new people sometimes-"

"No need to apologize, I completely understand. My husband was the same way." She swallows a gulp of wine after her words as if the subject makes her uncomfortable. I sip from my glass as well. The awkwardness slowly grows between us. I attempt to shut it down with a change of conversation.

"So, about that gossip you promised me..." She turns towards me as if she's been waiting for me to ask that. She smiles devilishly before she starts talking.

"Ok, so Vella is a small place, but it's *very* entertaining…" She goes on to talk about the biggest town personalities, who they are, and what they've done. I listen to her as long as I can before her conversation loses my interest. Honestly, her definition of juicy gossip is a regular day in Atlanta. I guess my face finally tells on me because she suddenly gets quiet.

"Wow, sounds like a lot happens around here." I attach a fake laugh to my statement, and she smacks her lips.

"It's ok. I know things aren't as exciting here as they are in a big city like Atlanta." I look at her sideways after her statement.

How the hell did she know I was from Atlanta?

"How did you know that?"
"Know what?"
"That I'm from Atlanta?"
"Oh, you told me." She looks away and sips from her glass. I lean up to sit my wine on the table.
"No, I didn't. I've never mentioned that to you."
"You did, when I came over and welcomed you to the neighborhood, you told me where you and your husband were from." I make a confused face as my mind tries to travel back to the day she's referring to. I comb through our conversation in my memory, but not once do I remember talking to her about Atlanta. I eventually give up on trying to figure it out.

I had to tell her. How else would she have known?

"Anyway, do you have any questions about Vella? How do you feel about the town so far?" I hump my shoulders as if I'm unsure.

"Actually, I have yet to leave the house besides for a walk or two. Every time we need something for the house, Ray usually goes and gets it." Liz nods her head slowly.

"You take walks? Where do you walk to?"

"Well, so far, I've only been up and down this block for the most part. I did walk around the corner once, but those scary ass buildings freaked me out." She leans up with a serious expression.

"You walked down Killer Kane Drive?" A puzzled look covers my face.

"Did you say Killer Kane Drive?"

"Yes, I mean, it's called 'Kane Drive', but 'Killer Kane Drive' is what the locals call it now. That whole strip of buildings is said to be cursed." My eyes get big with intrigue. I turn my body to face hers after grabbing my wine again.

"Way before I was born, those factories used to be the heart of this town. They employed most of the men that lived here at the time, and they were single-handedly responsible for the financial stability of Vella. They were run by a man named Kevin Kane, and I heard he was a mean old bastard. He was very hard on his workers, which made his company's productivity unmatched. No other factory far and wide could compete with Kane Industries. That was until the murders happened." I make a terrified expression. She sips her wine slowly.

"It was nearly Christmas and Kane had his employees working hard just like he did every holiday season. The men were exhausted. They weren't spending time with their families, some of them were working 20-hour days, it was super stressful and chaotic. So, one night, a bunch of them just snapped. Around 13 or so employees went around the plant and started killing other employees for no real reason at all. There were about 150 workers there that night, and only a third of them got away without injury. They slaughtered, bludgeoned, and beat many of their co-workers to death. They even noosed Kane and hanged him from the top of one of his buildings. It was horrific."

I swallow hard after her unbelievable story. I barely have a voice when I ask:

"So, what happened after that? What happened to the killers?"

"We didn't have a real police force at the time, so they had to call in the state officers for a crime of that magnitude. The men who hurt or killed their workmates were still standing on Kane Drive when the squad cars pulled up, covered in blood. I heard they didn't put up a fight or anything. Most of them claimed they didn't even know what happened. The others said it was some unknown force controlling their bodies like they were puppets. It's all crazy either way you look at it."

"Damn," I mumble, still in disbelief. She nods her head as if she agrees.

"But that wasn't the craziest part. Everyone claimed to see 13 attackers, but when the police showed up to make an arrest, it was only 12 of them. The men insisted it was no one else, but those that survived swore they saw a dude in the front leading them dressed in all black. To this day, no one knows who the 13th guy was, if there even was one. The sad part about all of this was that half of the women that inhabited Vella were suddenly widowed with fatherless children, and since they didn't work, they couldn't fend for themselves. Many of them perished. It was unbelievably devastating." My eyes well up at the thought. Liz takes a deep breath.

"So, it's a saying around here that the 13th man was really a demonic curser. They think he put a hex on the men of this town, mainly the married ones. Majority of those that survived were single, and most of the ones that were killed were married. It's still folks around here that think that's true." She humps her shoulders, "And I can't disagree with them. My husband left me, too.

CHAPTER NINE

I open my eyes slowly, noticing quickly that I have the worst headache I've had in a long time. The haziness clears from my vision. My eyes get big once I realize that I have no idea where I am. I sit up suddenly, finally recognizing the beige and white decor at Liz's place. I look around the dimly lit room quickly.

When the hell did I fall asleep?

I check around for my cell phone, but rapidly remember that I never brought it with me.
"Fuck!" I whisper aloud, "Ray is going to kill me!"
The two wine glasses on the table next to the two empty wine bottles catch my eye. I try to think of the last thing I remember, but after Liz introduced that second bottle of merlot, I can't recall much of anything.
I stare towards Liz's hallway that I'm sure leads to her bedroom. I want to tell her I'm leaving but deem the gesture a bit weird. Besides, I don't like wandering around stranger's homes without their permission, anyway. I haven't so much as been to the bathroom in her place.
I stand up slowly from the couch while holding my throbbing forehead. I stumble to the side slightly as I move towards the front door. I walk out into the pitch-black

darkness of night, closing the door quietly behind me. I look both ways down the empty, lightless block before stepping off her porch. I begin dragging my woozy body towards my home.

The sounds of the still night creeps me out a little. The darkness here is more defined than that in the city, so I can barely see a few feet in front of me. I want to pick up the pace, but I'm suffering from a massive hangover, which honestly, is somewhat weird.

Wine has never made me feel like this before.

"Why would she just leave me on the couch like that?" I wonder to myself. I figure she was trying to be nice by letting me crash, but I wish she would have woken me up to go home instead. Now Ray is going to be extremely worried.

I hope I didn't get him too bent out of shape. The last thing I want to do is disrupt his already fragile mental state…

The spookiness of the night makes me think about the story Liz told me about the murders at Kane Industries. The fact that a town this small is holding a secret that big is a little hard to comprehend. What if the men here really are cursed, husbands in particular? Was it really a good idea for mine to move here?

"Britney! Oh my God! Where the fuck have you been?!" Ray yells as I approach our house. He was standing outside pacing back and forth nervously in front of the door. He runs towards me and gives me a hug, "I was so fucking worried about you!"

"Sorry, babe. I went for a walk to Liz's and had too much to drink. I forgot my phone, so I couldn't call-"

"You went for a walk and didn't let me know?" He asks after we make it inside the house. I close the door with a sigh.

"Yes, I did, but I thought I'd be back before you would even notice." Ray makes a face as if my explanation was offensive.

"Before I would notice? What are you trying to say?"

"I'm saying that lately, you've been distant. I hardly lay eyes on you anymore, and having a real conversation with you? Forget about it!" Ray folds his arms before breathing forcefully from his nose. He takes a step towards me, causing the hairs to raise on the back of my neck.

Even though I don't want to believe it, I'm terrified of my husband.

"You know how hard it was for me to get this job, right? Do you remember how many applications I filled out before I was able to get one interview? How many interviews I had to sit through uncomfortably while people secretly judged me after finding out I was in the nuthouse? How demeaning it was to basically beg the company I work for now to give me a chance?"

I look down embarrassingly. Ray did work damn hard to find a good job just so I could stay home and practice for our family's future. He went out every day looking for a career after they released him from the hospital. He was hired for a salary position at a prestigious company a little over a month later.

"Yes, I do. I'm sorry, Ray. I just miss you, that's all." Ray sighs before taking me in his arms. He kisses my lips sweetly.

"I know you do, baby, because I miss you, too. I guess I can understand where you're coming from as well. We did move away to get to know each other better and

finally have a normal life, but it's hard to do that when we hardly see each other." He kisses me again, "How about this? How about I take off tomorrow, and we do something romantic, just me and you?"
I blush at the idea. He grins back.

"Ok, that sounds nice."

"It will be, and after we eat a nice dinner together, I can have you for dessert."

CHAPTER TEN

Ray leaves the house to pick up a few items for dinner. I watch him through the kitchen window as he jumps in his all-black Explorer and pulls off. I sigh before looking back down at the vegetables on the chopping board. For some reason, he never asks me to go with him.

I wonder why not?

I slice up a head of Romaine lettuce for our salad. I think hard about how weird things have been since we've moved here. I never leave the house anymore, Ray is too busy for me suddenly, and I have yet to see a single soul in our neighborhood besides Liz…

And the man in black, of course.

"Ouch!" I shout after the knife sharply slices across my index finger. I stare at the blood oozing from the nasty cut. I rush over to the sink to run cool water over it. I watch the blood-streaked liquid gather near the center of the sink before it disappears down the drain. The sight of the red bodily fluid takes my mind back to my days volunteering at the psych ward. I close my eyes tightly once the memory starts playing like a movie in my head.

"So, I see you've made a new friend," Nurse Maggie spit out in a facetious tone. She watched me walk out of the rec room after talking with Ray. I sighed while moving past her, "Even after what I told you about him killing his girlfriend, you're still entertaining the thought of being with him? Child, you must have a death wish or something."

I stopped in my tracks after her words, deciding to defend the man that would soon be my husband. I faced her with folded arms. "No one can be judged by their past mistakes. We all do things we're not proud of." She smacked her lips, but I ignored her, "Ray has changed. He's sweet, and loving, and we're going to get married soon."

The nurse's eyes grew with shock after my statement. She shook her head at me. "You may feel that way now, but you won't feel that way for long. Follow me, I have something to show you."

Nurse Maggie turned around to walk down the hallway. I hesitantly followed her lead. She stood in front of an office with a door labeled "*Dr. Monroe*". She looked down the hallway before opening it with her key.

"Come on," she whispered, sliding in the entrance quickly. I followed suit and closed the door behind me. She walked over to a tall file cabinet in the corner.

"What are you looking for?" I asked after watching her flip through papers for a few minutes. She pulled a folder from the drawer right after my question.

"Why don't you come over here and see for yourself." I took a few steps towards her as I read the name on the front of the folder:

Raymond Dennis

I shook my head with disagreement.

"This is wrong. We shouldn't be in here." Nurse Maggie forced the file into my hand.

"Look, Dr. Monroe is gone for the day, so you won't get caught. I just think you should know what you're getting yourself into when it comes to Ray. Just think of this as an early wedding gift." Nurse Maggie chuckled obnoxiously before walking towards the exit, "Make sure you close the door behind you when you leave."

I watched her walk out and swallowed hard with nervousness. The truth was, I did want to know what I was about to get myself into, I was just too chicken shit to find out. His description of his heinous killing spree was vague at best. If I *really* wanted to know what happened, I had to read it for myself.

"No Brit, this is wrong," I tried to convince myself initially. I sat the folder on Dr. Monroe's desk to pace the floor. I walked a small, straight line repeatedly while staring at the thick pile of paperwork. I reluctantly picked it back up.

Even though I knew I shouldn't have, I opened the folder anyway. A small picture of Ray was stapled to the top right part of the page. I skimmed over the words underneath it quickly, reading over his several diagnoses as if I knew what they meant. I slowly turned the page. After a while, I found myself leaning on the desk as I read through Ray's childhood like it was a novel.

"Abusive father, drunk mother, no siblings…" My eyes became glossy once I found out how sad his circumstances were as a child. I turned the page again.

"Oh my…" My mouth fell open after I spotted a pile of pictures. I sat the file on the desk while keeping the photos in my hand. Tears trickled down my face every time I looked at a new image.

If my stomach wasn't empty, I'm sure I'd vomit.

"How could someone do another person like this?" I asked the air. I gawked at dead body after dead body sprawled all over different floors in his ex-girlfriend's home. Two men were found in the kitchen, both with several stab wounds to their bodies. One man was lying on his back with wounds to his neck and chest, while the other was stabbed mostly in the back.

Two women were discovered in the bathroom with one lying on the floor by the toilet and the other slumped over the wall of the tub. I covered my mouth once I spotted puncture wounds in one of the victim's faces. The one halfway in the tub was stabbed so many times in the back, big chunks of her flesh were hanging through the rips in her shirt.

The last picture was that of his old flame, Amanda Laneer. I nearly boo-hooed after seeing the condition of her body. Not only was her throat slit from ear to ear, but her head was barely attached to her body. Her eye sockets were nothing but pools of blood, like he slid his knife blade inside of each one of them-

"Baby, you didn't hear me knocking?" Ray asks after walking in the door with his hands full. He startles me from my bloody daydream. I stare at him with glassy eyes.

"Uhm, no, I didn't. Sorry." He sits the bags on the table before spotting the cut on my finger.

"Brit, what happened? Are you ok?" He rushes to my aid, "Here, let me see." He pulls my finger from underneath the water stream to get a closer look at it. He walks me to the bathroom to retrieve the first aid kit.

"You have to be careful, babe," he advises, wrapping my wound up carefully. He looks at me once he's done.

"Knives are dangerous, Brit, especially when you're not paying attention to what you're doing. You could have really hurt yourself."

CHAPTER ELEVEN

Yesterday with Ray was nothing short of amazing. It felt like old times when he and I ate dinner together with no distractions. He didn't step foot in the basement one time, and he hardly touched his phone at all. He and I talked and connected like we did when he first got out of the hospital a few months back. Any bad feelings I had about our new environment instantly melted away when I stared into his gorgeous eyes; And of course, after we ate a wonderful dinner…

He kept his promise and had me for dessert.

I'm floating on cloud nine today. Even though Ray woke up this morning and went straight to his work area, I didn't mind. We had such a perfect date last night that I don't think I'm going to complain about much of anything for a while. If we can make time to connect with each other like that once every week or two, I can see us easily living happily ever after.

I walk past our bookshelf situated in the corner of our living room. A book I haven't read in ages catches my eye, prompting me to curiously stop in my tracks. I slide it from between its neighboring novels. I stare at the cover.

"I can't believe I bought a book with four topless men on the cover," I say aloud with an embarrassing chuckle. I read the title and author's name:

Devul "D", by Ruby Wright

My eyes get big after recognizing the name on the cover. The white book sitting on Liz's table was also written by this author.

"*I wonder if she already has this book?*" I ponder. I quickly decide to call her to find out. I walk into the bedroom to grab my cell phone. I find Liz's number in my contacts, and then press the call button once I reach it.

"I'm sorry I missed your call. Please leave me a brief message and I'll get back to you as soon as possible-" I hang up before I hear the beep. I glance at the time after ending the call:

1:33p.m.

"*Maybe she's at work,*" I assume as I sit the book on my nightstand. "*I'll just wait for her to call me back.*"
                                    ***
I wake up suddenly from a nap I wasn't aware I was taking. I sit up in bed after noticing the time on the clock:

5:45p.m.

"*That was one hell of a nap,*" I think with a rub of my eyes. I spot the book sitting next to the clock that I sat there earlier.

"Liz," I mumble before checking my phone. I look slightly surprised when I don't see a missed call from her. When I was over there the last time, she kept mentioning repeatedly that she really wanted us to be friends. She was overly adamant about us being chatting buddies, but now that I think about it, I haven't heard from her since I passed out on her couch a couple of nights back.

I decide to call her again, but this time, the phone doesn't ring before it goes to her voicemail. I make a confused face. I slide on my shoes quickly. I step out my front door and proceed to the end of my walkway. I check the mailbox near the curb before glancing in the direction of Liz's place. I notice her car in the driveway and assume she's home.

That's weird, why isn't she answering the phone, then?

I run inside the house and open the basement door. "Ray, I'm going for a walk!" I shout. I close the door back before hearing a reply. I check my purse for my keys, but I don't see them right away. I hump my shoulders nonchalantly.

They'll pop up eventually.

I leave the front door unlocked when I head out of the house. I speed walk towards Liz's place, making an early decision to be back home before dark this time. I stare at her old, Chevy Malibu as I climb her porch's steps. I knock at the front door. I stand there for about 30 seconds before knocking again. Another 30 seconds pass, so I knock harder. I step away from the door to stare inside of her curtained window. There are no lights on inside as far as I can tell. I walk over to her door again.

I twist the doorknob and make a surprised face once I realize the door is unlocked.

"*People don't lock their doors in small towns,*" I remind myself as I slowly step inside of her home. I look around curiously.

"Hello? Liz! It's me, Britney," I announce before closing the door. I pause and wait for a response, but I never receive one. I reach for the switch on the wall with the room lighting up immediately afterward. My eyes roll over the white and beige colors again, but stop once I spot the two wine bottles and wine glasses we were using the last time I was here.

"What the-" I mumble, walking over to the familiar scene. I pick up the wine bottles and stare at the labels.

"These are definitely the wines we were drinking." I put them back where I got them with my antennas raising higher than they were a few seconds ago.

Liz's house is immaculate. There's no way she left those dirty glasses and empty wine bottles sitting there like that.

I turn to face the dark hallway that I refused to walk down before. I swallow hard, opting to call out to her one more time before moving through her home without permission.

"Liz! Are you back there?!" I shriek with a shaky voice. I step cautiously towards the black room at the end of the short hallway. I gawk inside of the dark bathroom to the right before rubbing my hand on the wall in search of the light. I flick the switch up, revealing another spotless space. I check the empty shower quickly before stepping backwards into the hallway. I face the spooky bedroom again.

"Liz…" I say so low, that I'm barely able to hear my own words. I stand at the room's threshold, deciding to stick my hand inside to feel for the light before I commit to going in. The light clicks on, and I sigh with relief. The room is clean and neat, resembling what a nice hotel room looks like when the guests first arrive. I finally walk inside.

"Liz, where are you?" I ask the air. I spot a cell and keys sitting neatly on her dresser. I walk over and pick up the phone.

"It's dead," I mumble, after pushing the home button a few times. I eventually sit it back down. I stare at the keys next, and besides a single house key and a Chevrolet car key, there's nothing else on the ring. I scratch my head while taking steps backward. I retreat to the hallway, remembering to turn off the lights in each room that I turned them on in. I head for the front door and open it. I face Liz's puzzling and inexplicable interior one more time with a sigh. "I don't know what's going on, but I hope Liz is alright."

CHAPTER TWELVE

I spend the next few days worried about Liz. I've called her phone several times, but it is still dead. Her car has been sitting in the same spot since I was down there last, and there seems to be no movement going on at her house at all.

I'm starting to think something bad happened to her.

"Honey, what's wrong?" Ray asks, gawking at me while I stare out into space. I glance at him from across the dining room table.
"Nothing, really. Just a little worried about Liz."
Ray sighs at my answer before taking a bite of his meatloaf.
I cock my head to the side curiously. "Why the sigh? You really don't like Liz, do you?" Ray finishes chewing before responding.
"It's not that I don't like her, I'm just not in the right mental space to be inviting new people into our lives right now." I nod my head as if I understand, even though I don't.

Just because he can't handle friendships right now doesn't mean I can't.

"Well, what am I supposed to do when you're at work all day, then? Just go without social interaction?"

"Of course not. I just don't care for the way Liz carries herself. You hung out with her once and you were already too wasted to come home. I wish you'd introduce yourself to another neighbor instead of putting all of your energy into being friendly to her." My mouth falls open slightly.

"Other neighbors? What other neighbors, Ray? Have you noticed that no one else seems to live on this block but you, Liz, and I? I haven't so much as seen a mailman come down our street! Besides us and the man in black, I'd swear we were the only people in Vella-"

"The man in black?" Ray asks, sitting his eating utensils down to give our conversation his undivided attention. I nod my head yes slightly.

"Yes, the man in black that haunts Killer Kane Drive. He's said to have cursed the men of this town-"

"Wait a minute, wait a minute... Back up. Hauntings and curses? Where are you getting this shit from?" I look somewhat embarrassed at the thought of revealing my source. He rolls his eyes at me.

"You let Liz convince you that there's a man around the corner that hangs out in old ass buildings and puts curses on men? Please tell me you're joking. You must be joking!" He gets angry as his last words leave his lips, causing me to jump slightly once they're said. I look down at my plate nervously.

"Please, Ray. Don't get mad. You're right, it's just a story." Ray gives me an apologetic glare before rushing to my side of the table. He gets down on his knees in front of me.

"Hey baby, I'm sorry to yell. Look at me; I'm sorry." My gaze buries itself in his. He smiles while caressing the side of my face.

"I keep telling you, you don't have to be afraid of me. I will never do anything to hurt you." I nod my head as if I understand. He smiles lovingly at me before kissing me softly on the lips. He stands up slowly and proceeds to his side of the table. We both prepare to eat again.

"Why don't you start writing again? I remember you telling me that you used to love to write stories. That seems like the perfect hobby for you right now." I grin at the idea, mainly because I used to love creating fiction, especially as a kid. I'd spend hours in my room everyday writing down anything my mind could conjure up. My friends used to be so impressed with the characters I could come up with.

Boy, those were the days.

"You're right, babe. Writing isn't a bad idea. I think I'll start tomorrow."

***

Last night was the first night since I saw Ray's hospital file that I could sleep past three in the morning. I wake up at around seven, feeling highly accomplished when seeing the sun rays beaming through the blinds on the windows. I smile hard as if I'm proud of myself.

I'm finally putting Ray's murderous past behind me.

Ray is already out of bed, which is nothing out of the ordinary. I strut to the bathroom with a different stride, brushing my teeth and emptying my bladder while I'm in there. I am so full of positive energy today, I could burst.

Today is officially the first day of the rest of our lives together.

I stroll into the kitchen and realize that Ray has already made me breakfast. *"A boiled egg and a bagel,"* I say with a smile. It might not sound like much, but it's a gourmet meal for Ray. He never cooks anything. He'd burn salad if he could.

I pick up the bagel before resting my backside against the kitchen sink. My top teeth sink into the cream cheese, causing me to make a weird sucking noise to remove the thick substance from my incisors. I bite, and then chew the thick bread while looking around. I imagine two small children, a boy with my peanut butter brown skin and a girl with Ray's eyes, running around the sofa while chasing each other playfully. I grin at the possibility.

Fuck "possibility". That's definitely going to happen. Ray and I will be starting a family very soon.

My eyes land on our bookshelf as Ray's words from last night play in my mind.
"Why don't you start writing again?"

I sit my breakfast down and walk towards the wooden shelves. I begin searching for my leather writing journal.

"Where is it?" I ask the air, sliding my finger past book after book. I move down to the second shelf, but I still can't find it.

"Where…" I say again, right before my finger comes to a screeching halt. My hand drops like it weighs a ton. "What the hell?"

"Pure, by Ruby Wright," I read, sliding the book slowly from its space. My eyes get big with a stunning realization:

This is Liz's book!

I stare at the front of the novel confusedly, and then at the back cover. I check it's neighboring book, recognizing "Devul D" as the story I was going to let Liz borrow a few days ago.

"Maybe I borrowed it from Liz," I think immediately, but dismiss that explanation quickly. When I was going through my books days ago, this one was not up here.

A white book would've stuck out like a sore thumb. So where...

I stand in one spot as if I'm stuck to the floor. Every explanation my mind tries to create gets shut down quickly by logic. I conclude that the only way this book could have made it on this bookshelf is if someone else put it there.

But who?

I haven't seen Liz in about a week, and Ray...

How could Ray do something like this?

I stare off into space, and then back down at the book again. I open it and flip through its pages. I flip through it until I make it to the end. I pause once I see red writing on the last, blank page.

"PLEASE HELP ME! HE'S GOING TO KILL ME!"

CHAPTER THIRTEEN

My eyes well up with tears while I read the message over and over again.

He's going to kill her?! Who is he?!

My sights quickly cut to the open basement door. My chest heaves with heavy breaths after panic sets in. Even though I don't know who *he* is, the first "he" that popped in my mind was Ray.

But Ray is my husband and I love him! He promised me he would never hurt anyone else again…

I begin arguing with myself internally. My heart and my mind take turns screaming at each other. My heart wants to believe all the things Ray has said to me since I've known him. All the promises he's made to be the best version of himself that he can possibly be, but my brain keeps yelling the same thing repeatedly:

ONCE A PSYCHOPATH, ALWAYS A PSYCHOPATH!

"Britney, just calm down. You're jumping to conclusions," I whisper to myself after taking a few necessary deep breaths. "This message could be a hoax for all you know, and even if it isn't, why does your husband have to have something to do with it? Liz did mention that she has an estranged husband. Maybe she was talking about him."

I close the book finally after I successfully convince myself to relax. Besides, there's a bigger question that needs to be answered:

How the hell did her book get here in the first place?

I finally spot my journal on the third shelf and carry it to my room. I open the brown, leather notebook to a blank page. I pull the top off my black pen with my teeth and spit it on the bed.

"I must be missing something," I think, deciding to write down everything I remember about Liz, starting from the first time I saw her outside watering her grass. *"Did anything seem weird about her?"*

I speedily write down all the events that took place, starting with her waving at me when I walked past her house our second day in town and ending with her and I having a drink at her place. I stare at the sloppily written list, reading over what I jotted down carefully. There are a few things that stick out to me somewhat:

1. *She baked my husband's favorite cake.*
2. *She mentioned I was from Atlanta, even though I'm unable to remember telling her that.*
3. *She told me about a town curse that may or may not be true.*

Her gifting my husband's favorite cake flavor can just be a coincidence, but her knowing we're from Atlanta, that's too spot on to overlook. She claimed I told her, but I'm almost sure that wasn't true.

Where could she have gotten that information from, then?

After pondering for a few minutes, I come up with two possibilities: Either she Googled Ray and me, or she got the information straight from Ray. The latter is nearly impossible, so it *must* be the former.

I reach for my cell phone on the nightstand to Google our names, but it's not there. I look on the floor, and then in the bed. I make a confused face.

Where the hell is my cell phone?

I stand up to look around the bedroom. Afterwards, I search the living room, kitchen, and then the bathroom. After not finding it, I stand in the hallway with a distraught look on my face.

A phone just doesn't grow feet and walk away!

"Ray! Have you seen my cell?" I yell downstairs. I wait impatiently for him to answer.

"Sorry, baby, I haven't!" He shouts back. I smack my lips out of frustration.

"Fuck!" I exclaim, trying to recall the last place I saw it. "I called Liz's phone a few times, but that was a couple of days ago." I draw a blank after that.

I head back to our room and flop down disheartened on the bed. I take a deep breath while thinking hard about what seems to be going on around here. Chill bumps form all over my skin after coming to a realization.

If things are appearing and disappearing without reason, then that means there is someone, or something, in this house with us.

***

"Ray, I'm serious, you have to listen to me."

"Brit, I'm trying! But you're making it very difficult when you're not making any sense." I take a frustrated breath. He folds his arms and stares at me. I stand up from our bed.

"You saw the message in the book! I told you about my cell phone, and I think the same thing happened to my keys! I'm telling you; something is really wrong with this picture!" My pleas for help cause me to mentally unravel right in front of Ray's eyes. He wraps his arms around my waist lovingly.

"Baby, listen to yourself. You're getting worked up over nothing. You showed me writing in a fictional book that is vague at most. She could have written down a thought, or a phrase that she wanted to remember, or it could have already been there when she bought it. The possibilities are endless with that. And as far as your cellphone goes, I'm sure it'll pop up. This isn't the first time you've misplaced it." I let out a loud sigh before looking up in his eyes.

"Well, how did her book get here, then? And what about my keys, where are they?"

"I have no idea how her book got into our house. You claim you didn't borrow it, but I think you must have and forgot about it. And your keys were here until you took them down to your friend's place that night you came staggering home drunk. They're probably still down there." He gets quiet and stares at me as if he wants his words to sink into my brain. Once I don't respond, he kisses me on the forehead and walks towards the bedroom door.

"I'm about to hit the showers, and when I come back, I want that ass naked and in position." He winks at me sexily before disappearing down the hall. I would usually be thrilled by his sexual declarations, but he said something before that grabbed my attention more.

"My keys are probably still down there, huh?" I think. *"I guess I'll have to go down there tomorrow and find out."*

CHAPTER FOURTEEN

The sweat drips down my face. I kick the cover from on top of me. I flip to one side, and then to the other.

Fuck this. It's entirely too hot to sleep.

I sit up in bed and notice that Ray is missing.
        "He must be in the bathroom," I think, before glancing at the time on the clock:

3:32am.

I sigh with defeat.

For a minute there, I thought I was cured. I actually thought I was over Ray's violent past; I guess not.

        I climb out of bed and towards our bedroom window. I leave it open all the time to let fresh air in, but for some reason, it's closed now.

I wonder if Ray closed it.

"Maybe that's why I'm hot," I mumble, opening the window back to its usual position. I stare out into the darkness of the night as if I can see something on our pitch-black street. No movements, house lights, or anything. The block looks abandoned like it usually does. I can't say I'm surprised.

I start thinking about my middle of the night wakeups and shake my head disappointedly. Even though I'm currently up around three a.m. like I am most nights, it wasn't an awful nightmare that woke me. I got up simply because I was uncomfortable. Now that I think about it, I guess I'm making progress after all.

My eyes change focus, going from the view of the quiet street to my shadowy reflection in the window's glass. The modest glow coming from the bathroom light down the hall gives me just the amount of light I need to see myself. I cock my head from side to side as if I'm studying my face in the mirror.

I really should consider moisturizing in the morning.

My eyes suddenly focus on another person's silhouette that seems to appear behind me. I immediately assume it's Ray, but quickly dismiss the idea due to their outline being more feminine than masculine. My eyes squint at the image as I then assume that my sleepy vision is playing tricks on me. I concentrate on the figure until my eyes grow as big as saucers.

Is there really an unknown person standing behind me?

I spin around quickly when my assumption scares the shit out of me. My eyes catch a glimpse of a person fleeing my room's entrance in a hurry. I jump back when the movement startles me.

"Ray?" I speak out, carefully listening for a response before stepping towards our bedroom door. I don't get an answer, so I freeze in my tracks.

"Ray?!" I shout louder this time. I stand still for a few seconds.

Nothing.

I swallow hard with growing nervousness. I inch forward until I reach the hallway.

"Ray, where are you?" I question in a frightened tone. My feet carry me in the direction of the bathroom. I peek inside, but Ray is nowhere to be found. I reluctantly turn my attention towards the dark living room next.

"Ray!" I yell again. My voice trembles with growing fear. My steps soften as I emerge from the hallway to the space situated between the rooms. I look in the living room, and then towards the kitchen. I try to swallow the terror creeping up my throat when I still can't find my husband.

"Ray, answer me!" My voice cracks with desperation. My eyes cut to the open basement door. Against my better judgment, I head in the direction of Ray's cellar office.

"Ray, are you down there?" I notice a dim light shining from the lower level as if a TV or computer screen is on. The stairs creak with the rhythm of my footsteps after I bravely decide to investigate the source of the illumination. Ray's computer desk comes into view before I reach the bottom step. His computer is on, but once again, Ray is missing. I approach it after recognizing the article on its screen.

"Local man, age 27, accused of brutally slaying a group of friends at a house party"

The tears surface in my eyes like they do every time I see this newspaper clipping.

"What the hell is wrong with Ray? Why does he keep looking this stuff up?" I whisper aloud while reaching for the mouse. I click the [x] in the upper right-hand corner to eliminate the screen. The article disappears, but it's another screen minimized underneath it. I spot a familiar face, prompting me to enlarge it to get a better look.

"Liz?" I mumble, sitting down in shock in his office chair. I stare at the large picture of her that was purposely pulled up on a social media site. She's smiling for a selfie while sitting on her light-colored couch. I glare into her eyes as if she was really in front of me.

Why is my husband looking at pictures of our neighbor?

I gawk at the image as if it has me in a trance.

How did Ray find her private page? Why was he looking her up? How did her book get on my bookshelf? Where is she?

My arm rests on papers scattered all over Ray's desk. I glance down, recognizing them immediately as part of his horrible hospital file. I cover my mouth after gasping in disbelief.

How the hell did Ray get his hands on these hospital documents?!

My tears successfully fall once the overwhelming pages touch my shaky fingertips. I thought I'd never see this information again. I honestly hoped I wouldn't.

I've had enough nightmares about this folder to last me a lifetime.

I unwillingly flip through the scattered paperwork, trying my best not to read the statements that I know will make me sick to my stomach. I try to ignore the stack of bloody crime scene photos, but the picture on top draws me to them.

"This isn't a crime scene photo," I admit to the air. I stare at the unfamiliar picture of a beautiful woman with her arms wrapped lovingly around Ray. I flip it over to read the back:

Ray and Amanda. Thanksgiving Day.

I stare at the picture as if it's due to come to life at any moment. I've never seen an old picture of Ray, not even when he was a child. I didn't know he had any, especially of him with the woman he would later murder. My heart breaks for her not knowing her devastating fate. I wipe the newest tears from my cheeks after sitting the picture down. Liz's face on Ray's screen captures my attention again, causing me to make a puzzling face.

"Wait a minute…" I look down at Amanda Laneer, and then at Liz. I slowly hold the picture up to the computer screen.

"They look just alike," I breathe out as chill bumps form all over my skin. Their features are so similar, they could easily pass as sisters. My chest burns with the realization.

If I can notice it, I'm sure Ray noticed it, too.

"He's dangerous," I hear from behind me. I jump to my feet at an alarming speed. I stare at a dark corner behind the stairs, waiting for the unknown person to emerge.

"Who are you?" I ask nervously. Liz's face appears from the darkness a few seconds later. My mouth hits the floor, "Oh my God! Liz, what are you doing here? Where have you been?"

"He's dangerous, Britney, and you need to get away from him."

"What are you talking about-"

"You know exactly what I'm talking about!" She exclaims, causing my heart to jump with fear. She takes a few steps towards me, "Get away from him while you still can, or you will end up just like Amanda!"

CHAPTER FIFTEEN

"Baby, wake up," Ray says, shaking my arm lightly. I pop up like the Crypt Keeper from his coffin on the TV show, *Tales from the Crypt.* I glance at Ray, but then slide away from him once I see his face. He looks slightly taken aback.

"Brit, what's wrong? Are you ok?"

"What happened last night? Where were you?" I ask in a groggy voice. I look around our bedroom as if I have never seen it before, "And where is Liz? Is she still here?" Ray stands up from our bed slowly with a long sigh.

"I have no idea what you're talking about, which seems to be the running theme lately, but I just thought I'd wake you because you've been asleep for a long time. It's nearly one in the afternoon." Ray walks out of our bedroom just as my eyes grow round with disbelief.

One in the afternoon?

I jump up to follow him, "Why did you let me sleep so late?"

"You seemed tired," he responds, without bothering to turn around to address me. I place my hand on my forehead when my confusion sets in.

"Ray, we need to talk." He pauses in his tracks as if he'd rather do a million other things than chat with me. He eventually turns around to face me.

"If it's about Liz, or my job, or your lonely feelings, it can wait. I have to go into the city today and pick up a few items for work. I can't cater to your frivolous needs right now." I make an offended expression with a tight arm fold.

Frivolous needs?

"Wow, well I'm sorry if my emotional concerns seem juvenile to you. You won't have to worry about me bringing up any of the aforementioned things to you ever again!" I turn to walk away, but he grabs my arm. I jump with fear.

Is he about to hurt me?

"Baby, I'm sorry, I guess I'm just a little cranky from being so tired, that's all. Work is draining me, plus I couldn't get any sleep last night because you were tossing and turning all night long. I was really worried about you." He makes a concerned face, causing my tense body to relax. He leans in and kisses my lips, "I'm sorry for being so grumpy. How about I grab us a pizza and we pig out and watch horror movies when I get back?" He steps his tall body closer to me sexily and I blush.

"Yeah, that sounds like a great plan."

"Then, after that, we can…" He whispers naughty acts in my ear, and I giggle. I shove him playfully in the chest.

"I don't know about all of that. We'll just have to see, won't we?"

***

I watch Ray's truck back out of the driveway and stare at it until it disappears from view. I toss my hair in a ponytail and make sure my shoes are tied tightly.

I've been waiting for this moment ever since he mentioned he was leaving a couple of hours ago.

I rush down the stairs and straight to his work desk. Everything is neat and orderly now, not disheveled like it was last night. I sit in his chair and start going through his drawers.

I couldn't have dreamt all of that, could I?

My fingers go through stacks of paperwork, but none of it refers to his hospital stay. I sigh after realizing that his hospital file is no longer here.

But it must be here… I saw it!

I grab his computer mouse and shake it from side to side. The computer wakes up and reveals a picture of him and I on his first day out of the hospital. He was hugging me so tightly from the back that I could barely breathe. He looked so happy, like he was excited about having a second chance at life. I was excited, too. The man of my dreams was finally all mine. I didn't have to share him with that godforsaken hospital anymore.

"What are you doing, Britney? This is Ray, your husband; You know him. You know he'd never do any of the crazy things you're accusing him of doing," my subconscious whispers. I lean back in the chair as second thoughts creep into my mind.

What if I'm wrong about all of this? What if I really did dream it all?

I cover my face with my hands.

"Amanda," someone whispers from behind me. I turn around quickly after realizing I just had a flashback of Liz's voice. My chest heaves with terrified breaths. I stare at the spot where Liz was standing last night...

[In my dream?]

"Fuck this, I'm sure his ex felt the same way about him that I do before he killed her ass," I mumble to myself, staring at his computer screen again. I notice it's locked with an eight-digit pin, but I have no idea what it could be. I type in his birthday, then my birthday, and then our anniversary date, but nothing seems to work. I give up before I lock his work computer indefinitely. I sigh with defeat. I stand up frustratedly and look around.

"There has to be something..." I say aloud. I walk around slowly, allowing my eyes to skim over everything I see. My feet carry me to the big, black door situated to the far side of the basement. I cautiously walk up to it. My hand grabs the doorknob to open it, but it's locked, and I instantly remember that Ray keeps it that way.

And he's the only one with a key.

"Dammit!" I spit out. I release the door handle once I realize I've hit another dead end. I start to walk away.

"Help me!" I hear faintly. I spin around suddenly to face the door again. I rush over to it and wiggle its handle.

"Hello!" I shout, pounding on the thick metal this time. I pause in between pounds, listening hard for the presence of someone on the other side of it.

Nothing.

The tears in my throat choke me on their way up. They eventually gush from my eyes, allowing me to breathe again. I rush up the stairs and up to the bathroom, throwing up my salad I had for lunch. I wipe my mouth with a shaky hand.

"Either there's someone trapped in there, or I've officially gone crazy," I say to myself once I stand to my feet. I stare at my distraught face in the mirror.

I think Ray is back to his old tricks again.

CHAPTER SIXTEEN

I pace the living room floor for a half-hour straight. My mind is so jumbled up that I can't seem to create one meaningful or cohesive thought.

Liz… Her book… My cell phone and keys… The mysterious door in the basement… The hospital file… Liz and Amanda looking almost identical… RAY.
What does it all mean?

I'm being pulled in so many directions at once that my mind is exhausted. I want to believe Ray, but I also can't deny what my own two eyes have been seeing. Liz's book ended up on my bookshelf somehow and my items are still missing. If Ray wasn't the culprit, then it had to be someone else. Liz disappeared from her home about a week ago, but I'm sure I saw her in my basement last night. I just heard someone in that locked room down there a few minutes ago, too.

I think everything is finally starting to make sense now.

"But, why Ray? Why would you do something like this?" I ask the air as tears rush down my cheeks. I wanted to believe he was rehabilitated. I wanted to believe that his horrible past was behind him, but I guess him seeing someone that looks so much like his ex-girlfriend made all those terrible feelings come rushing back. He hasn't changed after all.

So, what will he do to me, then?

I decide quickly that I don't want to wait around to find out. I need to come up with a plan post haste. I must find a way to free Liz before it's too late and get us both as far away from Ray as possible.

But how?

"I need my fucking cell phone!" I shout angrily, speeding through the house with the mission of finding it heavy on my mind. I ransack the place as if my life depends on it...

Because it does.

I turn the house upside down before concluding that my phone can't possibly be in our home anymore. I've searched everywhere. He must've taken it.

Now, how will I call for help?

I start to panic after realizing that I moved to the middle of nowhere with a man that's killed more people than I slept with. It will take my family months before they notice I'm missing. I allowed him to isolate me from everyone and everything I've ever known just because I thought he was the man of my dreams. Nurse Maggie was right.

I should've stayed away from him.

"No! Fuck that! You can't just let him win! You can't give up that easily!" I pep talk myself aloud. I pace the floor again, staring out into the distance as if the answer is going to appear right before my eyes. I glance around the living room until my eyes land on my bookshelf. Liz's white book catches my eye, causing me to stop in my tracks.

"Wait a minute, Liz has a cell phone! I saw it sitting on her dresser in her bedroom," I think to myself, *"But it was dead."* I smack my lips frustratedly. I contemplate harder, *"But I think it was an iPhone just like mine! I still have my charger!"* I hurry to my room and snatch the white cord and base out of the wall. I head straight for the front door and speed out of it. I proceed down the walkway slowly, making sure Ray's truck isn't coming down the street yet. I jog towards Liz's house once the coast is clear.

It won't be long, now! I'm going to call the authorities, they'll rescue Liz, and then Ray can go back to the nut house where he belongs!

***

I take a deep breath before walking through Liz's unlocked front door. I click on the light like I did the last time, expecting to see the bottles and glasses still sitting out in the open like they've been for a week. I freeze up once my eyes take in a spotless living room setting instead.

"What the-" I start to ask, walking towards the table to get a better look at it.

I know for sure there were two bottles and two glasses sitting here! I saw them on two separate occasions!

I hurry to the kitchen to look for the missing evidence of our girl's night. I check the trash can for the wine bottles, but the bagless waste basket is both clean and empty. Not even a piece of paper rests at the bottom of the container. I turn around and face the cabinets, swinging them open to peer inside. There are dishes stacked neatly on each shelf, but there are no wine glasses in sight. I check all the cupboards before the confusion fully sets in.

What the hell is going on here?

I open the refrigerator to the surprise of empty, foodless shelves. Its interior is so clean, it looks like it is on sale at an appliance store. I take a step back after shutting its door. I'm trying my best not to freak out, but nothing is making any sense!

"Cell phone!" I shout to myself, deciding to stick to the task at hand. All the other craziness going on can wait. Every second I waste is another second that Liz must spend being locked up and scared. She doesn't deserve that kind of treatment.

I guess that town curse on married men is real after all.

I walk down the dark hallway to the house's only bedroom. I click on the light, instantly zooming in on the spot where I last saw Liz's cell phone and keys. I approach them with a determined stride, only to pause when a wave of overwhelming perplexity crashes over me. I pick the cellular device up with widened eyes.

"This- This in my phone," I stutter out. My bright pink and gold butterfly case leaves no room to dispute it. I press the home button and the screen lights up, "And it's fully charged!"

I stare at the bars at the top and notice I have no service. I promptly dial 911, but I hear "Sorry, your call cannot be completed as dialed. Please try your call again later." I make a puzzled face.

Aren't emergency numbers always supposed to go through?

I try to call the police three more times before getting frustrated and sliding the phone in my pocket. I grab the keys quickly and head towards the front door.

If I can't call the police to come to me, then I'll just have to go to them.

I race out to the old Malibu in the driveway. I pull at the door handle, and like everything else around here, it's unlocked. I hop in the driver's seat and gawk at the keys. My jaw hangs low once I realize that these aren't Liz's keys, they're mine.

"WHAT THE FUCK!" I scream out at the top of my lungs. My head begins to pound from the stress of the situation. I try to soothe the pain by rubbing my forehead gently.

Something is seriously wrong here!

Still determined, I begin searching the contents of the car. I look around the front and back seats, but I can't so much as find a hair strand on the spotless carpet. I search the empty glove compartment, and as a last resort, I flip the driver's sun visor down.

"Bingo," I say when a single key falls into my hand. I jam it in the ignition to start it up. The starter doesn't click, the engine doesn't make a sound, not even the car's interior lights come on. I try again, and again, and again, but get the same result every time.

Figuring the battery is dead, I pull the lever to pop the hood. Looking cautiously down the road for any signs of Ray before exiting the vehicle, I jump out of the car and rush towards the front of it. After feeling around for a few seconds, my fingers finally brush past the latch I need to lift the hood. I gasp loudly once my eyes take in the car's contents… or the lack thereof. The car is nothing but an empty shell. No engine, transmission, or radiator, just an empty, hollow hunk of metal.

"Oh God," I mumble, allowing the tears to fall from my eyes and hit my shirt.

I'm never going to get out of here!

CHAPTER SEVENTEEN

I rush inside of Liz's place and slam the door. My heart is beating so swiftly, I swear it's going to pound right out of my chest. I look around desperately for answers that I barely have the questions for. I have no idea what's going on, but I feel like I'm in a real-life episode of the *Twilight Zone.*

"How can the car be completely gutted?" I ask no one at all. I pace the floor a few times before pushing my mind to its limits.

"But Liz lived here. Liz had a life, a job. She drove her car every day... *didn't she?"*
"What am I missing?" I ask myself over and over again, "Because I'm definitely missing something." I pace until I can't pace anymore. I decide to sit on the couch to rest my tired legs. I look around the small house repeatedly, wondering how this place can look so unlived in suddenly.

I saw Liz watering the grass. I came down here and had a drink with her. She said she worked a lot, but she never mentioned if she worked from home or not.

"I assumed she drove her car regularly, but have I ever seen it move before?" I slowly shake my head no after realizing I haven't. I shove my face in my hands while letting out a frustrating sigh, "But how can that be?"

I think I hear a vehicle coming, prompting me to stand up abruptly and head to the window. I subtly peek out of it, wondering if it's Ray's truck that's about to ride past. My eyes are glued to the street until I notice the noise was a false alarm. No car ever came down the street.

"Wait a minute, no car *ever* comes down the street," I mumble shockingly. I stare at the other houses, realizing their cars never move, either. I take a single step back from the window. Chill bumps form all over my skin.

What if those cars are gutted, too?

***

Feeling like a criminal, I jog to the closest neighbor's house with a car in its driveway. I open the vehicle's door quickly and slide inside of it. I lean down while I check its interior, and just like Liz's car, the inside is eerily spotless. I check the visor for a key, and once again, a single key is stashed there. I try to start it up and receive no vehicular reaction. I shake my head unbelievably.

This cannot be happening.

I look back at the quiet house that stores this car. I make another bold decision while staring at it.

"Fuck it, you've come too far to turn back now," I tell myself as I hurry to the porch. I knock and wait for an answer, even though I'm almost certain I won't receive one. I walk inside once my certainty proves true.

"Hello?" I say loudly, and as expected, I don't receive an answer. I swallow hard when I notice that this house not only has the exact same layout as Liz's, but it's the exact same colors, too! The beige and white decor nearly chokes me with its Deja vu. The place is in immaculate condition, which seems to be a running theme around here. This house isn't being lived in…

None of them are.

    I lean my body against the front door when I start to feel faint.
    "I don't… I can't…" I start to whisper while shaking my head slowly. The tears trickle down my face once my body slides down the door. My butt hits the floor a second or two later. I look around at the cookie-cutter house through blurred, wet vision.
    "Where am I?" I wonder aloud. "What is this place?" I try to think back to the listing for the house Ray and I bought, but for some reason, I can't remember anything about it. I know it was my idea to move here, but the details about how we went about it are a bit hazy. I wipe my eyes with the back of my hand.
    "Maybe I'm dreaming," I begin to think. *"Maybe this whole thing is one big dream I need to wake up from."* I close my eyes and rest against the door. I sit there in a meditating state until I hear Ray's voice.
    "Brit!" Ray yells from a distance. My eyes pop open quickly, "Britney!" I scramble to my feet, standing with my back against the door again. My heart beats a thousand times per minute. I stand very still as if he can see me, even though he's somewhere outside. I build my courage up enough to peek out of the window. I see him moving towards Liz's house hastily. He hops on the porch and walks in.
    "Shit! I left the car hood up!" I fuss at myself after realizing I never closed it, "Way to let him know what you're up to, Britney!"
    I take the opportunity to rush through the house for an alternative exit. I hurry to the kitchen when I notice it

has a side door. I try to open it, but quickly realize that the door isn't a real door. It's simply an additional wooden structure that's been made to look like a door. I step away from the strange sight and head to the bedroom. I go straight for the window, but once again, it's not real. Its more wood carved in the shape of a window with glass panels inside.

"No!" I spit out after it dawns on me that nothing around here is as it seems. The tears flow from my eyes again. I take slow steps backwards toward the hallway. I pause in fear once I hear the front door open.

CHAPTER EIGHTEEN

"Britney?" Ray says in a low tone. I turn around fearfully to stare in his direction, "What's going on, baby?"

"Stay away from me!" I shout as more tears gush from my eyes. He walks slowly towards me anyway, "I said, stay away from me!" He stops suddenly.

"Britney, what's going on? Why are you acting like this?"

"What did you do to her?"

"Do to who?"

"You know who, goddammit! What did you do to Liz?" Ray shakes his head as if he doesn't know what I'm talking about.

"Britney, I don't know any Liz-"

"Yes, you do! Stop lying! She came over and introduced herself to us, remember? She even made your favorite cake as a housewarming gift!" Ray puts up his hands as if he's no threat. He slowly proceeds towards me again.

"Britney, just calm down. We can talk about this. We can talk about everything if you just come with me-"

"No! I'm not going anywhere with you! I'm calling the police, Ray! You kidnapped her! You have her locked in the basement!"

"No one is locked in the basement," he tries to assure me calmly. I try to run past him, but he catches me easily, "Brit! Calm-"

I knee him in the balls, causing him to keel over in pain. I take the opportunity to speed out of the front door. I run in the first direction my body goes towards, hooking the corner once I reach it. Kane Drive becomes visible, and I stop in my tracks after realizing I'm running the wrong way. I turn around to take a different route.

"Britney!" I freeze once I see Ray hot on my trail. I start running again, darting inside of the first rundown building I can get to. I slow down once the spooky, abandoned factory sends shivers down my spine. I step over piles of debris as Ray enters the building as well.

"Britney, please, I just want to talk." I'm preparing to flee as he continues, "I thought you loved me? I thought you trusted me? I thought I was the man of your dreams?" I hesitate. I finally turn around to face my husband. His hazel eyes burn into mine as the light from the sun shines through the factory's endless windows.

"I thought so, too, Ray, but that was before I realized that you haven't changed a bit. You're still insane!" I yell out my last statement and it echoes loudly throughout the massive building. He stares at me with disappointed eyes.

"Dammit, Britney! We were so close; do you know that? So fucking close!" He gets frustrated suddenly, rubbing his low haircut with his hand. He looks worked up, even though I'm not sure why. He gives me a serious glare, "We've run out of time."

"Run out of time? What- What are you talking about?" I ask curiously. He pulls out a cell phone I've never seen before and presses a button. He puts it up to his ear.

"Yeah, I'm sorry, but I really did try. I really did want to help her, but I can't." He hangs up the phone and places it back in his pocket. My curiosity grows tenfold.

"Who was that you called? And who did you try to help?" He gawks at me as if he wants to answer the question but doesn't know how. I walk towards him, "Was that call about Liz?"

"God, Britney! How many times must I tell you, there is no Liz!" He screams his serious words so loud, I jump once they're said. I stop in my tracks.

"Ray-"

"No, don't Ray me. Don't you fucking Ray me! Britney! Goddammit! You need to listen! There is no Liz! There never was! There is no Liz, no man in black, no marriage, no house; No nothing!" I stare at him with devastated eyes. I'm so confused that I can't speak. He walks up to me and grabs my shoulders aggressively, "Shit! I loved you, too! I fucking loved you! I can't believe I allowed myself to fall in love with a patient!" I shake his hands off me immediately before taking a step back.

"Ray, what the fuck are you talking about?" I'm so frightened by what's going on right now that I can barely breathe. He turns his back to me.

"It doesn't matter now. None of it does. You still won't admit what you've done, so they're going to make you pay."

***

"Ray! Please- Please stop! Please talk to me!" I follow Ray down Killer Kane Drive like a puppy following his master. He ignores me until I jump in front of him. "Please, Ray! Please! I just want to understand what's going on." He sighs before staring at me.

"Tell me about us." I look at him blankly.

"About us? What do you mean?"

"Tell me the history of our relationship. Tell me how we met."

"Well, umm, I was a volunteer at the hospital-"

"Wrong." Ray bumps past me and starts walking again before I get a chance to finish my statement. I jump in front of him once more and he rolls his eyes at me.

"What do you mean 'wrong'? You didn't even give me a chance to finish."

"Because I already know what you're going to say! You volunteered to care for the sick people at the psych ward and I was a patient there." I make an agreeing face.

"Yeah, but if that's wrong, then how do you know that?"

"Because you've told me that before, Britney! You've told me that 100 times!" He yells all his words as if he's extremely upset with me. He tries to keep moving, but I stop him again.

"So, if that's not how we met, then please tell me, how did we meet?"

"What's my name?" I look taken aback by the question.

"Why would you ask me something like that? Why wouldn't I know my husband's name?" I ask offensively. He folds his arms.

"Humor me, then, and tell me what my name is."

"It's Raymond; Raymond Dennis." He sighs before shaking his head no.

"Wrong again."

"No, but that can't be. My name is Britney Dennis-"

"Exactly! *Your* last name is Dennis, not mine!"

"But I thought I took your name after we got married-"

"If that were true, and if we really were married, your last name would be Monroe, not Dennis." My eyes get big at the information. He nods his head as if he can read my mind, "That's right, my name is Raymond Monroe, as in Dr. Monroe. I'm your doctor at Kane Mental Health Hospital."

CHAPTER NINETEEN

I'm so shocked by his declaration that my mouth hangs open. He finally walks past me successfully, moving towards the house that he claims we don't share together. I glance at the building where I saw the man in black emerging from when we first moved here. I become paralyzed in fear once I see him standing in the doorway again. My heart fills with terror when he starts coming towards me. I open my mouth instantly to shout Ray's name. He turns around to see what I want as I run full speed in his direction.

"It's the man in black! He's coming! You said he doesn't exist, but I just saw him with my own two eyes!" I try to run past him, but he catches me. He wraps his arms around me tightly to stop me from moving.

"Look again," he suggests. I try to wiggle from his grasp, but he holds me tighter. "I said LOOK. AGAIN." He uses a commanding tone this time, prompting me to hesitantly do what he says. I look behind me and see no one there. I stop fighting him and he releases me. I turn around fully to get a better look at the dilapidated buildings.

"But… but I saw someone." Ray rests his hand on my shoulder.

"Britney, there's no one there. There never was." The tears appear once a hopeless feeling comes over me.

I spin around to face him, "What's happening to me?" He lets out a worried sigh before taking me in his arms. He holds me lovingly like he usually does.

"You're coming to terms with the truth." I sniff after soaking up his shirt with my tears. We separate and I stare into his eyes.

"What truth?" He throws his head in the direction of the buildings.

"Look again." I read his eyes, deciding to trust him and follow his orders. I turn my body around to face the scene for a third time, causing a loud gasp to expel from my mouth. Ray wraps his arms around my waist from the back before whispering in my ear, "Do you see? Can you finally see it?" I nod my head slowly in disbelief.

"Yes… I see it. It's- It's the hospital. We never left it."

Ray takes a huge breath of relief after my statement. He spins me around to face him.

"I'm speechless! I never thought you would come to terms with reality! I thought you were going to see what you wanted to see until the very end! Wow!"

"What's happening?" I cry out, trying my best not to freak out completely. I glance over my shoulder to look at the hospital again. The old factories are still there, but they're directly behind the psych ward.

The psych ward I thought I was visiting but was really a patient at.

"I think your delusions are dissipating. I think I may be able to save you after all!"

"Save me?" I ask, following behind him once he suddenly walks speedily towards the house. He proceeds through the door, and I close it once we're both inside.

"Yes, save you… from your scheduled execution." He hesitates on his last words as if he didn't want to say them. My eyes grow 10 times their normal size.

Execution?!

"I'm- I'm going to be executed?"

"Yes, next week. Well, you were, unless I could get you to come to terms with what you did. I had until today to get it done, but I didn't think I was making any progress. I see now that something changed within you, but unfortunately, I already made that call to the director to let him know the outcome of your treatment. I told him you couldn't be helped. Shit! I must call him back!" Ray pulls his unfamiliar cell phone from his pocket and makes a call again. He holds it to his ear, leaving a voicemail message when he's prompted to:

"Hey, Mr. Wright. This is Dr. Monroe. Hey, listen, our social experiment subject has made a drastic turn for the better. I need you to call me back as soon as you get this." He hangs up angrily.

"Fuck! I hope he gets that message before he calls the executioner."

I stand there in a complete daze. My body goes numb as if it's tired of so many emotions flowing through it at once. I back up towards the sofa and flop down once I reach it. Ray watches me attentively.

"Do you think you're ready to face the truth?" He asks in a delicate voice. He kneels in front of me. I hump my shoulders slightly.

"I don't know," I answer honestly. If I'm facing execution, then I must be the orchestrator of something incredibly sinister.

I'm not sure if I can handle finding out what.

"How about this? How about we start from the beginning. Let's break down everything in sections. That way, you won't be overwhelmed and hopefully, by the morning time, you'll be ready to admit your wrongdoings and get your execution overturned."

***

"Let's go back to the last thing you remember before we moved here," Ray suggests while I sit at our dining room table watching him. He's cooking a steak dinner, even though I had no idea he could cook. I swallow hard before responding to him.

"Umm, I- I remember us being on the road, driving for hours before we got here. I remember stopping at a diner to eat-"

"Before that," he interrupts me to say. He sits two steaks on separate plates before laying a few pieces of asparagus next to them. He walks my plate over and places it in front of me. I thank him while he brings his plate to the table as well. He sits down before I can answer.

"Well, we lived in my tiny apartment in Atlanta after we got married. You were having a hard time getting a job because everyone knew what you did, so I suggested we move somewhere new to start over. We decided on a small town in Alabama." Ray chews his steak before speaking.

"What if I told you that none of that is true?" I hump my shoulders as if I wouldn't know what to say. He bites a piece of asparagus.

How can he eat at a time like this?

"Britney, first of all, we're not married. You've been in the mental hospital for five years, but I've only worked there for two. When I started treating you, you became infatuated with me, telling me I was the man of your dreams and that we were going to be together forever. No matter how many times I tried to correct you, you never changed your story. You were stuck on me." My face permanently displays a surprised expression. I don't want to believe what he's saying, I mean, how can any of that bullshit be true? He lays down his fork and knife with a loud sigh as if he can read my mind, "Ok, you don't believe me? Follow me, then."

Ray leads me to his workstation in the basement. He pulls a chair from the corner and places it next to his. He eases into his seat. I finally sit in the one next to his. He unlocks his computer quickly, revealing the picture of him and I. I stare at it suspiciously. He reads my facial expression.

"I had to make everything seem real for this to work. I even got a second cell phone line for this experiment."

"Experiment?" I question, realizing I heard him say that earlier. He turns his body towards mine.

"Yeah, off the record of course, and the first of its kind, thanks to me."

He smiles as if he's proud of himself. I fold my arms at his inappropriate boasting. My unpleasant reaction causes him to speedily continue, "Anyway, your execution date was swiftly approaching, and I just couldn't stand by and watch them put you to death; I cared about you too much for that. It's always been written in your file that if you could admit to what you've done, then you could be treated and hopefully rehabilitated after that. If not, then you'll be unpredictable and dangerous, and they'd have no reason to overturn the death penalty you received for your crimes. I knew how much you loved and trusted me, so I talked the director into letting me care for you in an unorthodox way. As long as I stayed on the hospital grounds, he gave me permission to do whatever I needed to do to get you to acknowledge your truth. I knew that if I gave it time, things would start to surface on their own. All I had to do was go along with the story you created in your mind. The rest would work itself out." I process his words before staring at the picture of him and I again.

"So, all of this was fake? All the intimate talks we had, the times you told me you loved me, the numerous times I let you inside of me?" A strong feeling of deception fills my chest. He turns away from me with ashamed eyes.

"I'm sorry, Brit. Things weren't supposed to go this far. Since we're talking straight up, I think it's only fair that I be completely honest with you. You weren't the only one in love in our patient/ doctor relationship. I fell in love with you, too. Even though I knew I could lose my license for this, I wanted to do this experiment, mainly to help you, but to help me, too. I think I wanted you to be mine just as much as you wanted me to be yours. Since that can never be, faking it seemed like the next best option."

CHAPTER TWENTY

I'm completely speechless right now. He seems to be, too. We stare into each other's eyes as if there's so much we want to say, but we're afraid to say it. He breaks our gaze to turn his attention back to his computer.

"Anyway, I have a few videos here of our first sessions." He clicks on a file saved to his desktop and my name pops up a million times. He scrolls up to the first clip. He presses it, and then presses play when prompted to.

"Britney Dennis, session one. The patient has an extreme case of amnesia and massive bouts of delusive episodes. She's violent towards others and is kept in solitary confinement. I'm going to see if I can get through to her. So far, no one has been successful," Ray says into a video recorder, before turning it in my direction. I gasp loudly once I see my disheveled appearance. I sat in a chair, restrained at the wrists, and looking to the side in a daze. My hair is all over my head, and I'm drooling so much, it's almost unbearable to watch.

"She's just coming out of heavy sedation, but I'm going to try to see if I can get something out of her anyway. Ms. Dennis? Ms. Dennis, can you hear me?" I don't respond to his calls at all. Tears form in my eyes while watching the uncomfortable clip.

"Ms. Dennis? Britney?" I finally look in his direction.

"You're beautiful," Is the first thing that comes from my mouth. Ray chuckles slightly.

"Well, thanks for that, but we're not here to talk about me, we're here to talk about you."
"Me? You want to talk about being with me?"

"No, Ms. Dennis, not being with you, just you." I rise from my chair as the terrible image of me makes me sick to my stomach. I rush upstairs and head straight for the bathroom, throwing up the lining from my empty stomach. Ray hurries in behind me.

"Hey baby, you ok?"

"I'm not your baby," I remind him while standing to my feet. I rinse my mouth out with water before wiping my face with a towel. He sighs at my words.

"I know, I'm sorry. I wanted you to be, though. I hope that counts for something."

"Yeah, I'll cherish the thought up until I take my last breaths before my execution." I storm past him, and he follows me again. He spins me around to look at him.

"I tried, Brit, ok? I really tried-"

"When Ray? All you did was stay in that basement or fuck the shit out of me! I never remembered one time when you mentioned an execution, or my past-"

"I was building up to it."

"Bullshit!" I try to walk away from him, but he grabs me again.

"Look, you saw you on that video! You were so fucking out of it! But look at you, now. It's the difference between night and day! I guess I just… I started to view you as a normal person so much that I forgot I was supposed to be treating you. I forgot I was supposed to be helping you remember. I forgot what we were here for." He wraps his hands around my waist like he did all those times when I thought we were together. I take a step away from him.

"Well then, do your job, Ray. Help me remember. Save me from my ordered death."

***

We walk down the makeshift street as the sun begins to set on the unofficial town of Vella. He thought it would be a good idea for us to get some fresh air while we continued our talk.

"What is this place?" I ask, looking around at the dark homes.

"About 100 years ago, these homes used to house the families of the hospital workers. This place was a thriving community once upon a time. There were way more houses than this back then. This is the last strip of street left. They were going to tear these down, too, but they decided to keep them up and remodel them for some reason. I thought they would be perfect for what I was trying to do with you. I decided to move us in the one house they never got a chance to remodel. I thought things would seem more authentic that way."

I glance towards the house I thought was Liz's and sigh heavily. He follows my stares.

"I think it's interesting you picked that house for your other personality to live in. That house is the only residence in this artificial community that has working electricity, besides ours of course." I glare at him after he uses the phrase, "other personality". I hesitate before questioning him.

"Who- Who is Liz?" He sighs as if the question is a complicated one.

"Liz is a woman you began seeing shortly after the murders. She was part of you, but also part of your main victim, Amanda Laneer. I think your subconscious felt guilty for your crimes, so it made her up." My throat begins to burn as he leads me towards the front door. He walks in, and I eventually walk in after him. He turns to look at me.

"What did you think happened in here between you and Liz?" My eyes go straight to the living room table that held the wine bottles and glasses.

"I came down here to visit her. She wanted to have a drink, so we did. We talked about this town and the curse tied to it. She told me all about the man in black." I walk over to the table in question. Ray watches me attentively, "You say that Liz wasn't real, but I'm almost sure those wine bottles were. What happened to them?"

"I came down here and cleaned up just in case someone from the hospital saw the bottles and glasses. Drinking is a no, no with your medication. The side effects could have been lethal." I think back to how awful I felt after the wine and cover my mouth. I flop down on the beige sofa.

"So, if there was no Liz to give me the wine, where did I get it from?"

"The cabinet," he answers, joining me on the couch. "Apparently, the workers from the hospital would come here on their breaks and drink, nap, have sex… whatever it is they wanted to do. And since this was the only house with electricity at the time, they favored this place. You must've got your hands on some booze they stashed here."

I take in his words, trying to process everything he's saying. I turn my body towards him, "And the man in black?"

He looks at me like that question scares him. He breaks our eye contact, "The man in black is someone you used to talk about often, even before your trial. Apparently, when the detectives interviewed you, you kept mentioning some guy in dark clothing that you didn't recognize. You said he was responsible for all the murders at Amanda's house that night, not you. You blamed everything on him."

CHAPTER TWENTY-ONE

I stare at the side of Ray's face with confused eyes. He finally finds the nerve to look at me, "But, during the investigation, there was no sign of another killer at the scene of the crime, only you. One set of bloody footprints, one murder weapon, one-"

"But that doesn't mean anything! What if there really was someone else there that night?" Ray places his hand over my mouth quickly.

"We're not here to debate the persons responsible for that evening. Your lawyer tried that during the trial and failed miserably. We're here to get you to face the truth about your crimes. You did in fact kill those people that night at Amanda's house." I stand up rapidly and head to the kitchen. I put water in a glass and slowly sip from it. Ray eventually joins me at the sink.

"Are you ok?" He asks me sweetly. I glance in his direction.

"What do you think?" He sighs at my facetiousness.

"I know this is hard to hear, but it's something that not only you need to process but remember as well. You have to literally recall that night and the details associated with it."

"Why?" I turn to ask him with tears in my eyes. He looks at me as if he feels sorry for me.

"Because, Brit, we never got a 'why' from you. We know that you and Amanda were good friends, we know that she was having some sort of party that night, but we just don't know what happened in that house that made you want to kill everyone there."

We stare at each other for what feels like eternity. I finally break our eye contact.

"What if I can't do this, Ray?" He lets out a disappointed noise.

"Well, they'll deem you unfit to live and shoot a bunch of shit inside your body that'll eventually make you stop breathing." I gawk at him after his inappropriate description. He humps his shoulders at my expression.

"I'm sorry, but I'm not going to bullshit you anymore. If you want to save yourself, then you have to dive headfirst into this thing. No hesitations or second guessing. You have to face this thing head on, and you have to do it right now." Loads of anxiety try to weigh me down. I turn away from him once the fear of the unknown sets in. He places his hands on the side of my face, forcing me to look at him again.

"Britney, I love you, and I need you to conquer this; For us." He leans in and lays a passionate kiss upon my lips. My tongue happily massages his as an inappropriate moment of lust sweeps over us both. He picks my body up and places it on the counter.

"Since this is our last night together as a married couple, we should enjoy each other's bodies one more time." Ray kisses me again before I can protest, and for the moment, my execution is the furthest thing from our now lust-filled minds.

***

We walk in silence down the dark, fictional street. I'm tucked snuggly underneath Ray's arm while we stroll together like a happy couple without a care in the world. It's not until the hospital comes into view that the realization of what we're really doing here punches me hard in the chest. My throat gets tight as we approach our make-believe home. Ray takes a deep breath before opening the door. He turns to engage with me before stepping in.

"Are you ready for this?" I stare fearfully into his eyes, nodding my head yes slightly. We finally walk in the entrance together. We stop as soon as we cross the threshold.

"There is another reason why I picked this house that I didn't tell you about." Ray walks towards the middle of the living room before turning around to acknowledge me again, "Can you guess why?" He looks around the room, causing me to do the same. I hump my shoulders.

"You said you wanted this experiment to be believable, so you moved us into the home that wasn't remodeled yet." He nods his head as if my answer is true, but not the one he's looking for.

"Yeah, of course that's part of it, but did you notice this house has a different layout than the rest? All the other houses are almost identical, but this one has its own unique look?" I nod my head, letting him know I noticed.

"So, come here. Let me show you something." He holds his hand out for me and I walk over to him. He spins my body around once I reach him so that we're looking in the same direction. He holds me tightly around the waist, "Look around with me."

He spins us slowly in a circle, allowing me to take in the bookshelf, living room furniture, dining room table, kitchen, and back around again. I shake my head confusedly.

"I- I don't know what I'm supposed to be looking for-"

"Shhh…" He says in my ear, "Concentrate. Just keep looking… Keep looking."

We spin around again, and I stare hard at the interior of the home. He spins us repeatedly until I think I hear voices, "You hear that?"

He stops our movements, "Hear what?" I step away from him quickly once I hear it again.

"That! Those voices!" I turn and glare at him seriously. He takes an eager step towards me.

"What are the voices saying, Brit?" I close my eyes tightly to hear better. I hear a woman's laughter, chattering amongst peers, glasses clinking, *fun.*

"I'm- I'm not sure. I can't make it out."

"Try!" Ray encourages. I listen harder.

"It's- It's a woman. She's talking about someone, and everyone is laughing."

"Who's the woman, Britney? And who is she talking about?"

"Me. She's talking about me."

"Why?"

"I- I don't know."

"Britney, why is she talking about you?"

"She's saying horrible things; Awful, terrible things about me!" Tears shoot out of my eyes. I begin to hyperventilate. Ray grabs my arms.

"Who's saying these awful things about you?"

"Amanda! Amanda is! They all are! They're laughing at me! They're all laughing at me, and they need to die!"

CHAPTER TWENTY-TWO

Ray wraps his arms around me quickly to calm me down. I cry loudly on his chest. He kisses my forehead softly.

"It's OK, baby. It's OK. Everything is going to be OK." I weep freely until I'm able to regain my composure. I stare at Ray through puffy eyes.

"What just happened?"

"You just had a reawakening through subtle physical suggestions." I make a weird face as if I don't understand. He spins me around again so that I can see what he sees, "At first glance, does this place seem familiar to you?"

"Yes," I mumble.

"What's so familiar about it?" I look around once more before putting together an answer.

"The colors, the furniture placement…"

"Exactly. Why do you think that is?"

"Because I've seen this layout somewhere before." Ray smiles with relief before disappearing rapidly down the basement stairs. He reappears in record time clenching a folder in his hands.

"I have something to show you." Ray removes a printed picture from his folder and hands it to me. The shock from the image makes my knees weak. I sit down on the sofa out of fear of falling. Ray eagerly joins me, "Brit, please say something."

"Wow," is the only word I can formulate right now. I stare at Amanda and I sitting on a couch that looks almost identical to the one I'm now sitting on with Ray. It has a bookshelf next to it with a small table sitting in front of it just like the one sitting in front of Ray and me.

"Our place is set up just like Amanda's." Ray let out another sigh of relief after my words.

"Yes! Yes, it is, and with a lot of hard work, I might add. It was tough finding pieces of furniture like the out-of-date ones that Amanda's adopted mom had."

I take turns staring at the picture and then at my present surroundings. The floors are the same color. He even found the exact same wallpaper pattern to put on our walls. My mouth hangs open, but no words come out. He takes a deep breath before handing me another image.

"Now, look at this one." My eyes take in the picture before my hands can grab it. Amanda's small kitchen and dining room are portrayed next, and again, it looks very similar to ours. I stare at our table, and then the table in the photo. Amanda is sitting at it while sporting a huge smile. I'm standing to the far right of the image with my back towards the camera. It looks as if I'm doing something at the kitchen sink.

Ray's stares burn a hole in the side of my face, "Do you remember taking that picture?" I slowly shake my head no.

"I don't."

"Tell me, do you remember anything about your younger days? Anything at all?" I look up at the ceiling as if the answer is going to fall from the sky. I stare at it until Ray speaks again, "What about your mother? Your father? Can you remember them?" I realize quickly that I cannot. Water builds up in my eyes instantly.

Who can't remember their parents?

"No. No, I can't." Ray nods at my answer before pulling out another picture.

"These are your parents: Caroline and Arthur Dennis. They're from a small town in Alabama, which is where you were born." My shaky hand takes the photo from him. My tears finally fall once I get a good look at my parents' faces.

"What happened to them?"

"No one knows for sure. The paperwork about them doesn't say much. All that I know is your father was an angry and abusive man that beat your mother every chance he got. Once you were a toddler, you started experiencing that abuse, too. Your mom coped with bottles of alcohol. She spent most of her days passed out on the couch. It wasn't until a neighbor found you wandering in the street one evening that the authorities intervened. After that, you were placed in foster care."

"My God," I whisper before covering my mouth with my hand. Ray places his hand on my shoulder.

"Your foster days were typical. You bounced around from home to home when you were little. When you were about 11, though, you met Amanda. She shared a home with you for a while. According to that foster family, you two were as thick as thieves. You did everything together, so it broke your heart when she got adopted around the age of 15. Your foster family said that you were devastated. You wouldn't eat or sleep after Amanda left. They even thought you were going to kill yourself at one point. That's when they reached out to Amanda's adopted parents and told them about your predicament. They started inviting you over on the weekends. Your mood seemed to pick up after that."

Ray stops talking suddenly as if it's my turn to speak. I look at him as if I'm not sure what to say, "Does any of that ring a bell?" I hump my shoulders as if I'm unsure. Ray stands up and reaches for my hand. I give it to him. He helps me to my feet.

"How about this: Let me step into the hallway so that you can take a really good look at this place. Walk around and take everything in. Try to remember, Britney. It's important that you remember."

I stare at him walking into the hallway until he turns around to face me. I take a deep breath before looking around the living room again.

"Ok, Brit, try to remember… try to remember," I keep whispering to myself over and over again. I flip to the picture of Amanda and I sitting on her parent's couch. I stare at it, and then stare at the sofa Ray and I just got up from. I hear Amanda and I gossiping like schoolgirls as a distant memory makes its presence known. I smile at the topic of discussion:

Boys.

"Amanda and I used to talk about boys a lot. We would sit right here and gossip about the boys in school. All of us teenagers went to the same school, you know? Our small town was set up that way." I giggle as the memory makes me feel kiddy inside. Ray's eyes fill with excitement.

"Oh, really? Well, what did you and Amanda used to talk about when you were in the kitchen, then?" He points towards it, and I look that way. I walk towards the dining room table and rub it slowly with my hand. I sit down in the chair Amanda loved sitting in all the time.

"Amanda would sit here while I cooked breakfast. I would listen to her talk about whatever crisis she thought she was going through at the time." I jump up suddenly and head to the refrigerator. Ray steps closer to me as I open it up, "Eggs over easy, three strips of bacon, toast and jelly;

coming right up!" I grab the eggs and bacon from the fridge. I carry the items towards the counter.

"Did you like cooking for Amanda?" Ray asks me calmly. I grab a pan from underneath the sink and place it on the stove.

"I liked doing everything for Amanda. She was my friend… my best friend! Whatever she needed done, I did." I turn on the stove burner to medium heat. I use a butter knife to scoop a piece of butter from its dish. It sizzles once it touches the hot pan. I swirl it around the pan slowly.

"Everything?" Ray inquires, stepping a little closer to me. I crack the first egg into the pan, and then the second.

"Yes. I cooked for her, did her hair, did her homework, ran her bath water-"

"Really? Well, did she do those things for you as well?" I don't answer the question. I flip the eggs on their yolks once they're done cooking on their backsides. I grab a plate from the dish rack.

"You know, Amanda always liked to eat her eggs first. Even though I thought it was weird, that was just the way she liked doing things." I turn around to sit the plate on the table. Ray gives me a concerned look.

"What about the way you liked doing things, Britney? Did you ever do things you liked to do?" I display a forced smile.

"Of course I did! I liked making Amanda happy, so whatever she wanted to do, I wanted to do, too."

CHAPTER TWENTY-THREE

Ray patiently watches me finish cooking with his arms folded in silence. I sit the bacon next to the eggs, and after the toast gets a hearty slather of grape jelly, I place that on the table, too. Feeling accomplished, I take a step back and glare at the meal. I grin at the food until Ray finally breaks the silence.

"Do you like bacon, eggs, and toast?"

"Huh? Um, yeah, kind of. I like scrambled eggs instead of over easy ones, though, and I prefer strawberry preserves." He stares at the food on the table and huffs loudly as if he doesn't want to say his next words.

"Well, who's food is that, then?" I make a confused face, "Because I don't like over easy eggs, either." I stumble on an answer, trying to process the situation. I finally snap back into reality. My hand slowly rises to cover my mouth.

"I- I have no idea what just happened. I don't know why I cooked that. I just got so wrapped up in the memory; I guess I got a little confused." Ray reaches out to rub my arm sweetly.

"Baby, it's OK. I want you to remember your past, but I want you to keep a firm grip on reality as well. It's important that you stay grounded throughout this process. If not, then you may slip back into a mindset that neither one of us wants you to be in."

I nod my head embarrassingly as if I agree. Ray picks up a piece of bacon from the plate and bites it.

"So, what else do you remember about your friendship with Amanda?" I hump my shoulders.

"I mean, that was pretty much it. I basically described our relationship in its entirety."

"So, what happened, then?" I stare at him as if I don't understand what he means. Ray asks a more detailed question.

"What happened that made your friendship take a turn for the worse?" I make an uncomfortable face.

"I- I can't remember." Ray glances at the couch. He walks towards it while signaling for me to join him.

"You said that you and Amanda spent a lot of time sitting here and talking about boys. Did she have a boyfriend?" I flop down on the couch while thinking about the question. I eventually shake my head no.

"I mean, she had dudes that were interested in her, but she never settled down with just one."

"So, she dated a lot?" Ray inquires, sitting down next to me and grabbing his folder again. I nod my head slightly.

"Yeah, I guess you can say that."

"What about you? Did you have a boyfriend?" I blush at the question.

"Not officially. It was this guy I loved talking to, though. His name was Richard. He and I had English together. He used to love reading my stories." I get warm and tingly from the memory. Ray nods his head as if he understands.

"So, what stopped you two, then? Why didn't you and Richard date?"

"Because…" I start but stop in my tracks. My mind hits a roadblock almost immediately. Ray instantly notices my hesitation. He gingerly opens his folder and pulls out another picture.

"Is this Richard?" He questions, showing me a picture of a nice-looking guy in a football uniform. I confirm with a head nod that it is. I rub my finger slowly across the photo.

"Wow, I haven't seen his face in ages."

"Did Richard have a girlfriend?" I hump my shoulders before fully contemplating the question. Ray makes a noise of disapproval.

"Brit, you're going to have to do better than that. I really need you to think about this." I close my eyes as I force my brain to carry me back to a time I can barely remember. I see Richard's handsome face smiling at me, and I see me smiling back. I see him carrying my books down the hallway with our shoulders touching every other step. I remember us kissing after school in a hallway that was rarely used. Then, I remember him walking me home...

"No. He couldn't have been dating anyone. Our relationship was a little too romantic for him to be dating someone else."

"So, you were his girlfriend, then?"

"I guess so." Ray has another picture in his hand as if he already knew what I was going to say. He hands it to me.

"Well, why did he go to prom with Amanda, then?" My mouth falls open as if I want to answer the question, but I'm not sure how. I stare at their coordinated outfits while they stand in front of a limousine.

"I- I don't know." Ray sighs as if that's an unacceptable answer.

"Yes, you do know, Brit. Think! What happened that made Richard go with Amanda instead of you to the biggest dance in high school history?" I look around the room as it begins to close in on me. I slam my face in my hands, taking deep breaths as I try to fight off the overwhelming feeling growing in my chest. I begin searching hard for memories of Richard that are stashed away deep inside of my mind.

"I caught them," I blurt out, as soon as a memory becomes clear. Old feelings of anger surface as well, "I caught Richard and Amanda in her room one day. She was on top of him. The headboard was banging against the wall like crazy. They were having sex. She took his virginity."

CHAPTER TWENTY-FOUR

Ray's eyes get big as if he's shocked by what he's hearing. "Wow... I'm so sorry, Brit," he says in a sympathetic tone.

"We were saving ourselves for each other, Richard and me. We were supposed to go to the prom together, dance the night away, have an amazing time, and then make sweet love to each other underneath the stars at our favorite meeting spot near the creek. That's what we thought would have been the most incredible end to our special night. We wanted everything to be perfect." My eyes fill with tears from the hurtful past. Ray gives me an apologetic look.

"I know this is painful, and I'm so, so sorry that happened to you, but we have to keep going." I wipe the first tear that rolls down my cheek, "So, did you confront them when you caught them?" I shake my head no.

"I mean, I didn't have to. When I walked in on them, they both looked dead at me. Richard tried to push Amanda off him, but Amanda sort of pinned him down. She stared at me with the coldest stare, as if she wanted me to catch them like that. I was too devastated to speak."

"So, what did you do?"

"I turned around and left. I gathered my things and walked out the front door. I didn't stay at her house that weekend, or any other weekend after that."

"Really? So, that was the end of your friendship?"

"No. She called me the next day like nothing happened, talking to me about what her adopted parents were doing for her for prom. She talked on and on about her dress, her limo, *her date*... She talked nonstop about herself like she always did."

"And let me guess, you listened?" I sigh at his judgmental tone.

"I mean, she was my best friend. *My only friend.* Of course, I listened." Ray sighs as if he's secretly disappointed in me.

"And who did you go to the prom with, then?" I look away from him as if the answer is going to embarrass me.

"I had no other love interests, so I didn't go." Silence lingers after my pathetic answer causes the awkwardness in the room to grow tenfold. Ray glances at the time on his watch.

"It's late. Even though we have a lot to get through before daybreak, I still think we need some time to regroup. I must try to get in contact with the director again; plus, you need to take your pills. I haven't given you your evening dose yet." I look at him bewilderedly.

"I'm glad you brought that up. I meant to ask about what you said earlier. You mentioned that the wine I drank caused an adverse reaction to my medication, but I can't recall taking any meds at all."

"Yeah, that's because I've been sneaking them to you; Usually in your drinks with our meals." I make a confused face.

"I don't remember that-"

"Hints the word, sneak." I smack my lips at his response. He grins, "The main goal of this experiment was to make you feel as 'normal' as possible, but your mental state was still very much my primary concern. You were doing so well on the psych meds that I dared not stop them. I did seize your sleep meds, though. Sleep deprivation is always a key catalyst to slight mental dysfunction. I wanted to irritate your mind, not break down its main healthy mental structure that we've been working so hard to build."

"So, that's why I've been waking up at weird times of the night?" He nods his head yes.

"It was important that I gave your mind the room it needed to remember your past, so I stopped assigning your sleep meds a week before we left the hospital. Ever since then, you've been complaining about nightmares that wake you in the middle of the night. I could tell your mind was trying to remember, but your subconscious, in its usual protective fashion, decided to project the cause of your trauma elsewhere." Ray points to himself. I give him an apologetic glare. He holds his hands out as if he doesn't want me to apologize for anything. He stands up and heads towards the kitchen.

"It's OK. I honestly expected it. That's usually step one in situations like this. You start to remember pieces of a terrible crime, but the heinous nature of the incident makes it hard for your mind to come to terms with your capabilities to perform such actions." He removes the entire kitchen drawer and sticks his hand inside of the space that the drawer occupies. He pulls out a small, clear bag of pills. He puts water in a glass after putting the drawer back in its designated place.

"I knew you thought I was a mass murderer before you left the hospital. I was surprised that you were able to recall the tragedy so quickly. It was a promising start." He walks towards me with the medication and the water, "If you could remember the actual crime, then it was only a matter of time before you remembered that it was actually you that committed it."

***

"So, you think you're ready to continue?" Ray asks as soon as I open my eyes. I raise my head from his shoulder while wiping the drool from my mouth.

"What happened?"

"Your meds make you drowsy once they first enter your bloodstream. It's perfectly normal."

"How long have I been asleep?"

"A couple of hours."

"And you just sat here and let me lay on you that long?" Ray smiles at the question.

"I mean, I dozed off for a second, too, but yes… yes I did. You seemed comfortable." I grin at his kind words, "But, with that being said, we must continue. I was able to get in contact with the director, but he needs hardcore proof to submit to the state for them to reconsider your execution. We must meet with him first thing in the morning, so we need to make sure you're comfortable with presenting the whole truth about your crimes, the reasoning behind them, and a sincere promise that expresses your willingness to do what it takes to change."

I swallow hard after his words, realizing how major and incredibly scary this whole situation is.

If I don't get this right, then I'll be kissing my black ass goodbye!

"OK, so where do we go from here?" I ask nervously. Ray takes a deep breath before pulling out his next piece of photographic evidence.

"Here," he says, slowly placing the picture in my hand. My stomach instantly turns as soon as the bloody image registers with my vision. "Do you recognize this guy?" Ray asks, pointing to the young man sprawled out on the kitchen floor in a pool of his own blood. He's been stabbed in the back a couple dozen times. I swallow the forming vomit in my throat while shaking my head no.

"What about him? He points to the next guy. The salty water gushes from my eyes with my hand planted firmly around my mouth. I slowly lower it once I'm ready to speak.

"It's Richard," I cry out in a stressed tone. Ray nods his head sadly.

"Yes, it's Richard. He was at Amanda's get-together that night, and unfortunately, he didn't make it. You killed him."

CHAPTER TWENTY-FIVE

"What- I mean, why-" I shake my head with grief after realizing that my question won't come out fully. Ray places his hand on my shoulder in a caring way.

"I need you to remember what happened that night, Brit. What happened that made you want to kill those people? Why were those other people there in the first place? Was it some sort of party or study session? Were you even invited?" The tears continue to fall when Ray and I make eye contact, "Britney, what happened?"

I look down at the horrible image before closing my eyes tightly. I think about his questions repeatedly, but I can't find a definitive answer to any of them.

"Local woman, age 21, accused of brutally slaying a group of friends at a house party," Ray reads, causing me to open my eyes suddenly and look at him. He stares at me while holding a copy of a newspaper article with my face on it. I snatch it from his hand quickly. Confused tears flow while I read over the familiar article quickly. I stare at my picture afterwards, remembering all those times when I saw Ray's picture there instead.

"She came home for spring break. She'd been going to Spelman College for three years by that time, and her first couple years there, I'd visit her once every month or two. She stayed in the dorms the first year, and then a tiny apartment the second year. Things were good then." My face sports a surprised expression when the memories from the time in question begin flowing like an endless river.

"So, when did things go bad?" Ray asks quickly as if he's trying to keep my mind engaged.

"It all started when she met the girls who would later be her roommates: Mia and Lindsay. They started hanging with Amanda and me when I came into town. I still have no idea where she met those girls. It wasn't that they were completely unpleasant, but they were definitely an acquired taste. After a while, they started rubbing me the wrong way, so I asked Amanda if we could stop taking them along with us whenever we went out. I guess Amanda told them what I said, because the next time I went to Atlanta, all hell broke loose. Mia and Lindsay jumped on me as soon as I walked through the apartment door."

"Where was Amanda during all of this?"

"Standing right there. She's the one that let me in." Ray wears a taken aback expression.

"Wow. Well, what happened after that?"

"Amanda eventually broke it up after I was all bloody and bruised. Mia and Lindsay expressed very nastily that they were living in Amanda's apartment now, so I couldn't stay there anymore. Amanda never said a word, so I picked up my shit and left."

Ray stares at me as if he doesn't know what to say about that unfortunate incident. I reluctantly continue, "After that, I barely heard from Amanda. I tried calling her, but she hardly answered, and when she did, those bitches were always in the background. I hung up every time I heard their voices. Her and I didn't talk for six months after that. It wasn't until spring break was approaching that I heard from her again. She said she was coming home for a visit and wanted to link up with me, and it would just be me and her. It wasn't until I showed up to her parents' house that night that I realized she was lying to me."

Ray's eyes get big with intrigue, "Are you talking about *that* night?" I nod my head yes. I close my eyes while recapping what happened that deadly evening.

"I arrived at Amanda's, feeling all giddy at the thought of seeing my best friend again. She opened the door, and I hugged her like I've never hugged her before. I missed her terribly. Like I said before, she was my only friend." I sigh at the sad truth, "After I stepped in the house, my eyes spotted Mia and Lindsay, even though they weren't supposed to be there. They were sitting right here, right on the couch." I gesture to the spots where Ray and I are sitting, "They snickered as soon as I saw them. I turned around immediately to leave. 'Don't go! I promise, they won't bother you', Amanda said before I could walk out of the door. I turned around to face her and read the sincerity in her eyes. I believed her, so I stayed. Unfortunately, that was the wrong choice for everyone involved."

My mind halts out of fear of what comes next. My hands start shaking terribly. Panic and anxiety explode in my body. My throat burns when the evil truth tries to come out of it.

"Excuse me," I mumble, suddenly rushing to the bathroom. Vomit erupts from my mouth before I'm able to make it to the toilet. My acidic stomach contents splatter disgustingly in the sink. I throw up until I can't throw up anymore.

"Baby, are you ok?" Ray asks as he comes around the corner. His face frowns up at the repulsive sight of the yellow vomit. He turns on the bathroom faucet, helping me clean up behind myself. "Do you think you need another break?"

"No," I answer rapidly before cleaning my mouth out with water. "No, I have to finish this. I must get everything out in the open. I have to try to save myself."

***

Ray refills my glass of water before rejoining me on the couch. He stares at me as if he's ready to listen whenever I'm ready to talk. I sip from my glass and sit it on the table.

"Everything seemed cool at first. For the first time ever, Mia and Lindsay weren't complete bitches, and we were actually able to have a regular conversation. Things were going really well until the doorbell rang. God, I wish that doorbell never rung." I shake my head slowly with glossy eyes.

"Take your time," Ray says sweetly while gently rubbing my back. I sip from my glass once more to stop myself from visiting the bathroom again.

"Amanda stepped to the side after opening the door, and that's when I saw him; It was Richard… Richard and his friend, Chris."

"Well, what were they doing there?"

"After Amanda let them in, Richard said something about him hearing she was in town, so he wanted to stop by to see her. He made a weird face once he noticed I was there, almost like he was just as surprised to see me as I was to see him."

"So, what happened next?" Ray asks impatiently.

"They came in and joined us in the living room. Everyone tried to play it cool, but the awkwardness was too noticeable to ignore. Eventually, Mia asked if everything was OK with me. It wasn't in a caring tone; it was more so in a nosy way. I lied and said it was. Lindsay disagreed with me instantly, insisting that something was definitely wrong with me. They looked at Amanda for validation. She looked at Richard, and then back at her roommates. That's when things went bad."

"How bad?" Ray asks interestedly. I pick up the picture of Richard and Chris lying dead on the kitchen floor.

"This bad."

CHAPTER TWENTY-SIX

"Whoa, back up. I know that's how things ended, but what pushed you to that point?" I sigh as if it's getting harder for me to talk about this. Ray aggressively digs in his folder and pulls out more pictures. "Look! Look at this shit, Britney! Look at what you did! Don't you think these peoples' families deserve to know why you did this to their loved ones?"

He forces images of dead bodies in my face. I knock them to the floor quickly, standing up after his actions begin to upset me. He's never talked to me this way, and I honestly don't know how to take it. I storm away from him and head towards the bedroom. He follows me.

"Look, baby. I'm sorry. I don't know what got into me. I guess I'm just a little frustrated because we're running out of time-"

"Buzz…Buzz…" Ray's cell phone starts vibrating in his pocket, interrupting his words. He looks surprised once he notices it's his secondary phone ringing instead of his main one. I stare at him while he pulls out the phone that he claimed he activated for the sake of making this experiment seem real. I snatch it from his hand quickly.

"Hey! Give that back!" Ray yells as he tries to take the phone from my hand. I run in the bathroom and lock the door once I'm inside. He pounds on it like a mad man. I stare at the name on the screen.

"Dr. Monroe?" I say loud enough for him to hear in a shocked voice, "I thought you were Dr. Monroe?"

"I am! Please! Please don't answer that call! I'm begging you!" My mind races back to the time I stumbled across him whispering on the phone in the middle of the night.

He claimed he was talking to Dr. Monroe, but if he's Dr. Monroe, then who the hell is this calling his phone right now?

"Hello?" I say in a low tone, closing my eyes with anticipation. I swallow hard when the feminine voice on the other end repeats me.

"Hello?" The unknown woman and I both sit in silence as if we're trying to figure out what to say next. The lady finally clears her throat.

"Well, if it isn't Britney. I haven't seen you in about what? Two weeks now?" I make a perplexed expression at the strange woman's claims. Ray finally stops beating on the door as if he knows it's already too late to stop me from finding out whatever secret he's hiding. I find the courage to respond.

"Who- Who is this?"

"Damn. You're still having a hard time remembering things, huh? I told Ray this would never work, but he insisted on running his little experiment, anyway. I knew he was biting off more than he could chew when it came to you. You can't be helped." My eyes get big once an overwhelming feeling of anger sweeps over me. The burst of emotion gives me the ammunition I need to speak my mind.

"And who the hell are you to draw that conclusion?" She chuckles obnoxiously, causing the unpleasant sound of her laughter to jog my memory perfectly.

"Nurse Maggie," I spit out in a disgusted tone. She gasps with surprise.

"Wow! I guess you can remember something after all." She giggles again. I roll my eyes at her unattractive disposition.

"What do you want?"

"Actually, I called to talk to Ray. Where is he?"

"Working," I reply in an irritated fashion. She sucks her teeth at my response.

"Not for long, dear. I heard you missed your deadline to qualify for becoming a normal person again. As of Monday evening, they'll be storing your body in the morgue. It's honestly a little sad. I've been caring for you since they locked your unstable ass up." She tries to ruffle my feathers, but I remember quickly that I've dealt with women like her before. I decide to let her words roll off of me.

"Like I said, Ray's busy. He's going to have to talk to you later-"

"Listen here, you crazy bitch! If you don't give that phone to my fiancé, you won't have to wait for Monday to meet your maker! I'll come back there to that house so fast, you..." My ears turn off after the word "fiancé" registers in my mind. I drop the phone from my ear once the term makes it too hard for me to comprehend anything else. Hurt tears stream down my shocked face. I unlock the bathroom door and open it slowly. Ray leans against the wall across from the bathroom, staring down at the ground as if he's too embarrassed to face me. I approach him with the phone out in front of me.

"Your fiancée wants to speak with you; but I'm sure you knew that already."

***

I sit on the couch looking at crime scene photos when Ray wraps up his very loud conversation with his soon-to-be wife. He was in the bedroom while he yelled at her for 15 minutes straight, even though he tried his best to keep their conversation private. After opening the room door, he approaches the living room cautiously.

"Brit, can we talk?" I don't look up at him. I can't look up at him.

My heart is too broken to do so.

"Sure, we can. I have to finish telling you about what happened that night-"

"I wasn't talking about that; I was talking about you and me." He sits down next to me. I stare at the picture of Mia and Lindsay's dead bodies instead of him. He notices what I'm looking at and makes a nervous expression. He's afraid of me, even though he's trying his best not to show it. I finally look over at him.

"They locked themselves in the bathroom that night. They thought that a locked door was going to keep them safe," I chuckle inappropriately. "A piece of thin wood would never keep anyone out of a room they really wanted to get in. That's why we don't have anything to talk about, Ray. You wanted me to find out about you and Nurse Maggie. If you didn't, you would have broken down the bathroom door just like I did at Amanda's house that night." Ray's mouth hangs open as if my comparison is hard to grasp. I ignore his troubled expression.

"So, like I was saying, Mia and Lindsay poked at Amanda until she finally opened up about what happened between her and Richard. 'But what does that have to do with Britney?' Mia asked in that bitchy tone she always used. Chris jumped in suddenly like his name was Richard, Britney, or Amanda. 'Oh yeah! Dammit, I can't believe I forgot all about what happened in high school!' Chris blurted out before running off at the mouth about everything he 'heard' happened between us three."

"That had to be unbelievably embarrassing for you," Ray throws out.

"You don't know the half. But anyway, that's how the 'let's bash Britney show' started. It went from them talking about Amanda stealing Richard from me and taking him to the prom, to Mia and Lindsay jumping on me and beating me up in Atlanta."

"And you sat there the entire time they talked about you? Why?" I hump my shoulders at Ray's question.

"My self-esteem has always been low. I used to think I deserved to be treated like that. If my own parents didn't want to be around me, then why would anyone else want to be? I guess that's why I held on to Amanda's friendship as tightly as I did. Now that I think about it, we were never really friends at all. People don't treat their friends like Amanda treated me." Ray nods his head at my words as if he agrees with them.

"So, what was the final straw?"

"Amanda started talking about how she used to dog me out when we were kids. She was boasting about how I used to do everything for her, calling me her maid and shit like that. 'You know what? It sounds like she was in love with you!' Lindsay joked and everyone laughed. Then, Amanda's eyes got big as if Lindsay's statement made something click in her mind. 'You know what, Linds, I think that's what it was! I was the first person in her life to show her any type of attention. Hell, her own family disowned her. Ever since we've met, she's been stuck on me like a lovesick fool. Her being in love with me would make sense, but I'm sorry, Brit, I don't swing that way."

CHAPTER TWENTY-SEVEN

"Ouch." Ray mumbles. I take a deep breath, trying my best to fight off the strong urge to cry. Ray carefully takes the photos from my lap, "So, give me a timeline using these pictures. What happened first?" He holds them fanned out in his hands like we are playing a game of cards. I slowly slide the picture of Chris and Richard's bodies from his grasp. I stare at it before I start talking.

"I excused myself to the kitchen, where I acted like I was grabbing a glass of water. Instead, I stood at the sink and cried my eyes out. Richard approached me after a while of me being away. He startled me when he placed his hand on my shoulder. He asked if I was OK, and I nodded my head as a reply. He then went on to explain how he never meant for the incident with Amanda to happen. It was me that he really cared about, but when Amanda asked him to come over that night I caught them together, he went anyway. He claimed she seduced him, and he just wasn't 'strong enough' to fight her off."

I stare straight ahead with a blank expression on my face after my story takes me back to a mental hell I haven't visited in a while. I blink once, allowing a single tear to escape the pools of water that has gathered around my bottom eyelids. I brush it away before I continue.

"I asked him why I never heard from him again, then? Why did he not once try to apologize to me for breaking my heart? Why did he decide to go to the prom with her, instead? My back was still facing him when I forced out those questions. I remember using the huge butcher knife in the dish rack as a focal point while I waited for him to reply. The light coming in from the dark kitchen's entrance bounced off the shiny blade in a distracting way, glistening like a brand-new diamond. It was very... captivating."

I pause once I remember the sight, "Amanda put on *Drake's* CD while the silence between Richard and I lingered. I heard fun coming from the other room once the music started playing. Everyone was laughing and having a good time. No one seemed to care about what they had just done to me; The pain they had put me through. They used me as the butt of their jokes just to make themselves feel better about their pathetic lives. I was nothing to them at that point."

"Well, did Richard ever answer your questions?" I chuckle at Ray's inquiry. I catch another tear before it falls.

"He told me that he wanted to call me, but he didn't know what to say, and since I was already mad at him, then it was in his best interest to go with the girl that wasn't." I chuckle again, "Can you believe that? My heart got stomped on when I found him with his dick in my best friend, and the only thing he had to say for himself was 'Sorry, Brit, didn't know what to tell ya, so I went with the chick that wasn't angry'. Ha! The audacity!" Ray rubs my arm slowly to try to keep me grounded.

"And, what happened next?"

"Just at that moment, '*Worst Behavior*' by *Drake* started playing. Are you familiar with the lyrics to that song?" I look over at Ray while he shakes his head no, "Anyway, I start rapping the song in a melody similar to Drake's tone. I think about his aggressive lyrics a little longer before continuing, "It came on just at that moment when the knife's blade I'd been concentrating on seemed like the only answer to my problems. Richard kept asking me to say something, as if that bullshit reasoning he gave me deserved a response. After repeating himself for the third time, something just… snapped. I grabbed the knife, spun around, and plunged it in his heart before he ever got a chance to see it coming. He let out a weird shriek when the blade slid between his ribs. The shock of the whole thing showed painfully on his face. We both fell to the floor after that."

Ray tries to act like my graphic story isn't bothering him, even though I can tell by his red appearance that he's two seconds away from vomiting himself. He swallows hard, "OK, and then what?"

"And then, I kept going. I stabbed him over and over again. I remember thinking how hard it was to get the knife in his body at first, but it seemed to get easier as time went on. It was like the blood was acting as some sort of lubricant for the knife's blade or something." Ray makes a horrified face. I ignore it and continue my story as a strange feeling of pride comes over me, "I was just getting off Richard when Chris walked in the kitchen. He was stunned by the scene at first, shouted something about me being a crazy bitch, and then he turned around to run away. That's when I plunged the knife in his back, causing him to buck like a horse. I had to stab him a bunch of times to get him to go down. He was much stronger than Richard was."

"Ok, I think I got it," Ray says in a sickened tone. He fans out the remaining photos, prompting me to pick another one. I glance at my options before shaking my head no.

"Actually, the next thing I did is not in any of these pictures."

"Go on," Ray insists reluctantly.

"When I walked in the living room dripping in Chris and Richard's blood, Amanda, Lindsay and Mia completely lost their shit. They started screaming like wild banshees. Amanda tried to run for the front door, but I caught her before she reached it. I threw her towards her stereo system, which she hit before her forehead slammed into the wall. The impact knocked her out cold. Mia and Lindsay screamed even louder at the sight of Amanda hitting the floor. They darted down the hallway as soon as I turned around to face them. They rushed inside the first room they saw, which was the bathroom. They locked themselves in there, which I've already told you earlier." Ray stares at me as if he's trying to make sense of everything he's hearing. He shoots me a troubled expression.

"At this point, why didn't you stop trying to hurt these people? Did the fact that what you were doing was wrong ever cross your mind?"

"When I first attacked Richard, I was terrified. I felt like I was going to hell for what I was doing, but I physically couldn't stop. I was too emotionally distraught. When I stabbed Chris, it was mainly because he saw what I did. It wasn't until I straddled him from behind that I began to strangely enjoy myself. I felt like I was in some sort of euphoric trance, and that's when I saw him; the man in black."

"The man in black? Britney, I thought we went over this! Didn't I tell you there was no one else there besides you and your victims?" Ray asks in a fed-up tone. I look at him like he has no fucking idea what he's talking about.

"I thought I was the one telling this story, but I guess I'll let you take a crack at it since you seem to know more than I do about what happened that night." He smacks his lips at my facetiousness. We have a stare-off, but he doesn't respond. I roll my eyes at him, "Do you want to know what happened, or not?" Ray sighs angrily.

"Of course I do, but for future references, when we go in front of the board, don't mention the man in black."

CHAPTER TWENTY-EIGHT

"Where did I leave off?" I ask after returning to the couch with my recently microwaved steak and asparagus that I didn't have the appetite for earlier. For some strange reason, I'm starving, now. I sit down after placing the plate on the table.

"You were talking about Amanda being knocked out and Mia and Lindsay locking themselves in the bathroom."

"Oh yeah, that's right," I agree, sliding my steak knife back and forth to slice the meat. Ray watches in horror as if the piece of steak represents a human body part. I smirk at his reaction.

"I'm really freaking you out, huh? I bet you're glad that you're with Nurse Maggie instead of me for real, right?" Ray makes an embarrassed face but doesn't say a word. His body language is defensive, almost like he's worried about me taking my knife and stabbing him with it. I shake my head and release my eating utensils. They fall to the plate.

"Ray, I'm not going to hurt you, if that's what you're thinking. Was it fucked up that you made me believe I was your wife just so you could fuck me? Sure. Did your lies break my heart? Most definitely, but that's no real reason for me to cause you bodily harm. I was somewhere else mentally when I did those terrible things in the past. That's a place I'll never go back to again." Ray glares at me as if he doesn't believe me. I sigh at his paranoia.

"I'm sorry. It was never my intention to break your heart. I hope that one day, you'll find it in your heart to forgive me. Now, finish the story, Brit. What happened next?" He decides to keep it short and business-related. I can tell he's not liking me too much right now. He's not my favorite person at the moment, either.

It wasn't like we were going to be together, anyway.

"I stood there for a moment, watching Amanda sprawled out on the floor. Our entire friendship flashed before my eyes; the good and the bad. I wished shit could've turned out differently, but I guess I felt that way about a lot of things. At the end of the day, life happens, and it brings a bunch of terrible shit with it."

I grab a piece of asparagus and bite it before I continue, "Anyway, after my attention slipped away from Amanda's unconscious body, it went straight to the sounds coming from the radio. I know this might sound weird, but when Amanda bumped into the CD player, it messed up its playback. *'Worst behavior… worst behavior… worst behavior…'* was being chanted repeatedly from the speakers like a sinister mantra. I remember saying it over and over again while I hunted Mia and Lindsay-"

"Hunted?" Ray asks in a shocked voice. I stare at him confusedly.

"Wait, did I say that?"

"You did," Ray points out in an offended tone. I think about my last words quickly.

"Shit… maybe I did. I didn't mean for it to come out that way, it was just the first word I could think of to describe what happened. I remember walking towards the bathroom without telling myself to do it. The same thing happened when I kicked down the bathroom door.

Naturally, you, with your masculine strength and all, can knock down a door quickly if you really wanted to, but I shouldn't be able to. I mean, look at me, I'm petite as hell. There should've been no way for me to get through that door as quickly as I did. That's when it dawned on me: The man in black had taken over my body to execute those terrible crimes. All that I could do was watch helplessly as everything played out. It almost felt like I was viewing a horror movie."

Ray stares at me with a blank expression on his face. I can tell he's thinking terrible thoughts about me, and I can't say that I blame him. It hurts me deeply to watch him fall out of love with me right before my eyes; That is, if he ever really loved me in the first place.

He's been in a relationship with Nurse Maggie this entire time.

He fans out the pictures again without saying a word. I reach for the one portraying Mia and Lindsay's deaths.

"They begged for their lives once I made it inside. For the first time since I've known them, they were genuinely afraid of something, *or someone.* Their squatting bodies were squeezed between the toilet and the wall next to it. We stared at each other for a while without either of us moving a muscle. Their eyes went from me to the knife and back again. Then, I guess Mia found a shred of bravery because she slowly eased up from the ground. 'You don't have to do this,' is what I remember her saying. She eased towards me with her hands out in a peaceful way. I stared at her without saying a word, and once she got within a few feet of me, she lunged at me. My knife caught her right in the gut. She groaned out in agonizing pain. I pushed her and she fell across the tub. My blade slid in and out of her back until my arm got tired. I have no idea how many times I stabbed her."

Ray rubs his forehead as if he's stressed, "What was Lindsay doing during the attack? She never tried to help her friend?"

"She cried loudly in the corner near the toilet. She never even tried to get up. Killing her was the easiest kill of them all."

Ray points to the stab wounds in her face, "So, why strike her here?" I look at him with serious eyes.

"Because she was the one that talked too much."

***

"There's only one crime scene photo left," Ray points out before putting the other pictures down. He holds the image of Amanda's nearly decapitated body in front of me. I eventually take it from his grasp. I stare at it for a moment before speaking.

"Yeah, this is a tough one," I mutter, swallowing hard after my words. Tears rejoin my eyes once I realize I can no longer look at the photo without my stomach turning. Ray notices my reaction.

"Why is that one so hard for you to look at over the others?"

"Because Amanda was my best friend. I loved her." Ray picks up the picture of Richard and Chris.

"So, you didn't love Richard?" I hump my shoulders as if I'm not sure.

"I mean, I probably could have if he didn't fuck my best friend behind my back." Ray nods his head as if he understands.

"Ok, so let's finish this up. Tell me about Amanda's death." I look away from him and close my eyes. I take a deep breath before forcing myself to talk about it.

"Amanda was still knocked out cold when I came out of the bathroom. I stared at her lying on the floor as I approached her. I got on my knees next to her and admired her beautiful face. I've always known she was prettier than me, but I didn't mind. As long as she was my friend." My heart rate increases at the thought of what happened next. "I remember glancing down at the knife and it's messy appearance. It was smeared with the blood of the others, dripping almost. It was disgusting, but breathtaking. Poetic, even." I nod my head slowly at the unorthodox comparison, "All of those years of us being friends, and she never truly knew me. She never asked how I was doing, or if I was OK. She never once thought about my concerns, or problems, or feelings. She never, ever saw me!"

My hands begin to shake once a ball of fury tries to engulf me suddenly. Ray places his hand on my thigh, "Hey. Relax, Britney. Relax. Breathe. It's just a story." I glance at his face for guidance. He breathes deeply and signals for me to do the same. I do so until I'm able to calm down.

"I get it. You were very angry with Amanda for being a lousy friend. You didn't think she cared about you- saw you as you say. So, what did you do next?"

"I slid the tip of my knife inside of her eye sockets. If she couldn't see me, then I needed to make sure she never saw anything else again."

CHAPTER TWENTY-NINE

"Jesus, Britney!" Ray shouts in disgust after hearing my horrendous confession. I look over at him slowly.

"Well, you wanted to know." Ray turns his nose up at me.

"God, just hurry up and finish this shit already," he mumbles in a tone as if he's officially over this whole situation. He makes a face like he can't wait to get as far away from me as possible.

"Wow. You went from dying to know to wishing I'd stop telling you. My, how the tables have turned." Ray tightens his jaw like he's trying to hold back what he wants to say. I fold my arms tightly.

"Don't just sit there; Say it! I may not be your real woman, but I still believe I know a lot about your deceitful ass!" He stands to his feet quickly.

"Britney, what the fuck is wrong with you! How could you do some shit like this?!" He takes all the crime scene photos and tosses them at me. "And then, to hear you talking about this shit like it's normal? You can't be helped! There's no way in hell any sane person is going to overturn your conviction after listening to you talk about slaughtering these people in cold blood so nonchalantly!" He removes a tape recorder from his pocket and presses the stop button. I look confused.

"You were recording this?" I ask in a low tone. Ray's attention slowly darts toward the dim light shining through the window.

"Shit! And we're out of time!" He yells loudly. He hurries to the back of the house. I stand up hurriedly to follow him.

"Ray, why would you do that? Why would you record me saying those things?"

"Because Britney! You think they're just going to believe me when I tell them you confessed everything to me? You think they're going to simply take my word for it? Fuck no! I needed proof." Ray grabs his duffle bag from the closet and starts tossing his important items in it. I watch him, but I'm unable to move. The perplexity of the situation has me stuck. He moves around the room like a mad man.

"Fuck! I'll just have to get the rest of my shit later," he exclaims before walking out of the bedroom. He scurries towards the bathroom as if he's looking for something, and then the living room.

So many emotions are flowing through me, and I can't fully feel any of them. My mind constantly tries to make sense of all this:

Ray is not really my husband.
I am a dangerous mental patient on death row.
I've perpetrated some of the most heinous crimes known to man. And…
I'm probably going to die soon because of it.

Devastation finally consumes me after I realize I probably won't be alive past next week. Tears begin streaming down my face. I slowly walk around a swiftly moving Ray and stand near the front door. I would pack up my belongings, but there's no point.

I don't need luggage where I'm going.

     Ray finally stops moving when he approaches the basement door. He turns around to face me, "What are you doing over there?"

     I look confused by the question, "Wait- Waiting on you. I thought we were going back to the hospital?"

     "We are," he starts, swinging open the basement door, "But it's easier if we go this way."

***

     I follow him down the stairs curiously. He pulls out his keys, walking up to the big, black door a few seconds later. I hesitate slightly as we approach it. Even though Ray said that Liz never existed, I still can't help but to think about her being locked up in there. The cries for help from the other side sounded so real.

     I stare at him nervously as he unlocks the door. The door creaks open, revealing a long, dim corridor before us. I swallow hard at the thought of walking through it.

     "This tunnel leads us straight to the hospital," Ray says, stepping inside of it with me close on his trail. We walk at a steady pace down the spooky hallway. I turn around to look behind me, trying to get one last look at the life I thought was mine.

The house, the husband, the freedom…

All a lie. I sigh after the depressing realization kicks in. The sight of the house's basement gets smaller with every step we take. I turn around to stare at Ray's back after the sight becomes too tiny to see.

     "I was wondering where you were disappearing to in the middle of the night. I see you were secretly going back and forth to the hospital," I say in an awkward tone. Ray doesn't respond, making me feel more horrible than I did before.

My negative feelings spiral out of control with every step we take. Ray is no different than Amanda, or anyone else I've met in my life for that matter. He pretended he loved me, used me, and then threw me away like I was nothing. Now, I'm not even good enough for him to acknowledge when I'm speaking.

"You've never seen me, either. You're just like Amanda." Ray pauses after my old best friend's name leaves my lips. The old lights above our heads flicker scarily once he turns around to face me. He stares at me seriously.

"Is that what you think?" He asks in a terrifying tone. I've never heard him sound so sinister before. I take a cautious step back.

"Why are you sounding like that?"

"Like what?" He spits out quickly. He takes a slow step towards me.

"Like… evil all of a sudden? Demonic almost?" His eyes grow colder every second.

"Like a demonic curser, you mean?" My eyes get big after he uses the same words Liz used when she described the man in black. I take another step back.

"Ray, what's going on?" My voice shakes with my question. He continues to stare at me with his terrifying gaze. My legs speedily carry me backwards without me telling them to do so. He stands in one spot, not even bothering to chase me.

I turn around to run towards the house. I stop dead in my tracks once a woman's silhouette comes into view. She walks slowly towards me. I gasp loudly once her face becomes clear.

"Liz?" I mumble, feeling completely paralyzed by the sight of her, "I thought you weren't real?"

"I'm not," she says, right before a hard hit on my head makes everything go black.

CHAPTER THIRTY

My eyes open and take in the living room Ray and I just left from. I try to move but realize quickly I'm tied to one of the dining room chairs. Panic sets in instantly. I frantically bounce around in the wooden seat.

"Help!" I scream out at the top of my lungs. I wiggle relentlessly until a familiar voice rings out.

"Scream all you want. No one will hear you. No one lives here, remember?" Ray says after appearing from the hallway. My actions cease quickly at the sight of him.

"What is this?! What's going on?!" I cry out once the tears begin to flow. He continues packing up more of his things.

"Sorry about all of this, but this is what must be done. Too bad it had to be you." I make a confused face.

"Ray! What are you talking about?!" I shout frustratedly. Ray stares at me like he feels sorry for me. He approaches the couch that is near me and sits down.

"I can't believe this whole thing worked! I mean, for a minute there, I thought the whole concept was preposterous, but it really, actually worked."

"What did?" I ask confusedly. Ray glances at the hallway as if he's waiting for someone to appear. I follow his gaze and see Liz emerging from the bedroom a few seconds later.

"Oh my God," I say in a low tone.

"Surprise!" Liz exclaims facetiously. I stare at her as if I'm seeing a ghost.

"I- I don't understand," I admit. She sits down next to Ray.

"Oh sweetie, of course you don't." I look at her, and then at him.

"But you said she wasn't real."

"I said a lot of things, Britney." I stare emotionally into his hazel eyes before looking away. I begin sobbing as if my heart is broken. He walks over and kneels in front of me.

"I'm sorry, I really am, but setting you up was the only way I could save my sister."

"Sister?" I ask between the tears. Ray glances back at Liz.

"Yeah. Lizzie is my little sister. She's set to be executed soon, but now that you've confessed to her crimes, they'll have no choice but to set her free."

My eyes bounce from Ray's face to Liz's, and then back again. So much about what he's saying makes no sense at all!

"But how can that be! I remembered everything about those murders!" He stands up and begins slowly pacing the floor.

"That's because you were there that night, Britney, and you saw exactly what happened. You weren't the one holding the knife, however." Liz sticks her hand up and we both look her way.

"That'll be me."

Ray takes a step back and folds his arms, "Brit, you were right. You weren't alone that night. Lizzie is the man in black."

***

"But, why? I mean, how?" I ask, trying my hardest to connect the dots of his words, even though I'm having the hardest time doing so. He kneels in front of me again.

"The 'why' is because you're an overly trusting female that happened to be a suspect of said crime once upon a time; and the 'how'... well, that answer is a little more complicated."

"Gosh! I can't believe you still don't remember!" Liz blurts out in a shocked fashion. She shakes her head in disbelief.

"That's because of the drugs I've been giving her. She barely remembers anything before we arrived at this house."

"Remember what?" I finally find the courage to ask. Ray places his hands on my thighs.

"The truth," he answers.

"I think we should tell her." Ray gawks at his sister as if her suggestion is a bad idea. "I mean, why not? We've come this far. We've got the recording we need to make everything we've been telling everyone stick. Plus, once we get back to the hospital, you're going to pump her full of so many drugs that she's going to forget it all over again, anyway. Tell her! Please! I really want to see her reaction. I'm already free to walk as far as I'm concerned." Ray let's Liz speak her piece before letting out an unsure sigh. He turns to engage with me again.

"Do you want to know the truth?" Ray questions me hesitantly. I nod my head yes. He sighs once more before grabbing another chair and sitting it in front of me.

"Where should we start?" He asks Liz without looking over at her. She gets up and heads to the kitchen.

"The very beginning. That's where every story should start, I think." She grabs a plain bag of chips as if she's getting a snack before a movie. She eases back down on the couch.

"Ok, well, the things I told you about your childhood were true when you were a toddler. Your mom and dad really did neglect and abuse you, and you really did end up in foster care. After that, though, you did meet

Amanda, but not at a foster home. You were adopted by our parents." My eyes widen after his words. He nods his head to confirm that my thoughts are right.

"Yes, Amanda was me and Lizzie's biological sister."

CHAPTER THIRTY-ONE

"What?" Is the only word that comes to mind after hearing Ray's words. He rubs his hands over his face quickly.

"Yeah, Amanda was our sister," he says again, but this time, in a more hurtful voice. He shakes the thought of her away before his emotions get the best of him. Liz notices his hesitation, so she continues.

"You took to Amanda immediately when you came to live with us. Y'all became instant best friends. It's funny because Amanda was never that friendly towards me. She hated me," Liz adds, getting distracted by her memories suddenly. Ray jumps back in the conversation after staring at his sister with concerned eyes.

"When our parents adopted you, I was getting ready to go away to college. The only time we'd lay eyes on each other was when I came back for school break. Even then, though, I was barely at home. I hung out a lot back then." Ray makes an uneasy face with his words. Liz giggles at his actions.

"No matter how you try to make it sound, she's still our sister. You've been fucking our sister, Ray. That's disgusting." Her obnoxious laugh catches my ear. I realize suddenly that I've heard that laugh before…

But where?

"Shut up, Elizabeth! I did this to save you, remember?" Ray looks me in my eyes after his loud outburst, "Plus, she's not really our sister."

"Nurse Maggie!" I exclaim, after realizing where I heard that ridiculous chuckle from, "You were who I talked to last night! You said you were Nurse Maggie!" Liz smiles like she's proud of me for recognizing that.

"Yeah, that was me. I was just calling to check on my brother, but when you answered, I decided to fuck with you instead," she boasts.

"But you sounded just like I remember Nurse Maggie sounding." I look at Ray, "How is that possible?"

"I told you; all of this is complicated-"

"Because, I am Nurse Maggie," Liz expresses while talking over her brother. "I never would've come up with the idea if your Mother Teresa ass didn't start coming up to the hospital doing volunteer work. Insanity plea or not, they were still going to fry my ass for what I did to my sister and her friends. Seeing you, though, was like staring at a 'get out of jail free' card. All that I needed was a doctor familiar with hypnosis and hallucinogenic meds and a nurse to convince you of a story that wasn't true. Since I only had one of those people," she points at Ray, "Then, I had to be the other person."

***

"I'm confused," I admit as soon as Liz stops talking. She sighs while placing the bag of chips on the table. She stands to her feet.

"Alright, girlie. I'm about to break everything down for you. Are you listening?" I smack my lips at her facetious question. She smiles at my reaction.

"Ok, so when mom and dad first brought you home, the first thing I thought was 'Why in the fuck would they bring home another fucking kid when they already have three? This place is crowded enough.' But of course, the opinion of a nine-year kid holds zero weight, so I kept my opinions to myself. Since you and Amanda were the same age, they set you up in her room. You and her were inseparable after that. It was sickening." She makes a repulsed face.

Ray takes over the story, "As time went on, things started to change. Once Amanda got to high school, her attitude changed, not just towards you, but towards all of us." Liz nods her head as if she agrees.

"So, kill her?" I blurt out as if I'm not understanding the point. Ray and I look at Liz. She walks towards the bookshelf and skims over the books.

"Ray, I can't believe you brought all of this shit here. I thought mom and dad got rid of all their furnishings after they moved," Liz says, deciding to change the subject. She pulls out a book from its space and reads its back cover.

"They wanted to, but I asked them if I could have it. They didn't want to say yes at first, but I talked them into it. It's been in storage ever since. I don't know, I just wasn't ready to part with it, yet."

"Even if it does remind you of the time when your baby sister murdered everyone in your childhood home?" I butt in and ask sarcastically. Ray makes an uncomfortable expression while Liz makes an amused one.

"Not everyone. You're still alive," she corrects me. I make a curious face about her statement.

"Which reminds me of something else I wanted to ask: Why me? Out of everyone there that night, why keep me alive?" She turns my way after putting the book back where she got it from.

"Believe me, fake sister, it wasn't on purpose. The only person I would've ever spared intentionally was Ray. Everyone else, including mom and dad, would've caught my blade that night."

"Shut up. You don't mean that," Ray says in an offended tone.

"The hell I don't!" She responds, leaning on her brother's shoulder. He rolls his eyes at her inappropriate comments as she continues, "I didn't notice the side door was wide open until I got done carving up Amanda. Turns out, you ran to the neighbor's house and called the police. You told them you woke up to weird noises, quietly got up, and stumbled across me doing my Chucky shit with mom's favorite knife. You said you hid until you saw your chance to escape. So, I got arrested." She humps her shoulders before pacing the floor, "Of course, I blamed you initially. After all, you're no real relation to us, so it was a more feasible explanation if you ask me. But no! Mom and dad told the cops that I was most likely responsible for the mess at home, so I was tossed behind bars instead of you."

"Like forensics had absolutely nothing to do with that! You were going down for those killings regardless of what your parents said! My God, Liz. You're fucking insane!" I spit out aggressively. A shocked look covers her face as soon as the word, "insane", leaves my lips. She walks over and slaps me so hard, blood flies from my nose.

"Fuck you, Britney! I tried, OK! I tried to be 'normal'... whatever the fuck that means! I tried to be like everyone else, but everyone else's lives sickened me! My mom and dad hated each other, but they walked through life arm and arm like no one could tell they were fucking rotting inside! And my sister was so up her own ass that she didn't give a fuck about anyone else's feelings, and her lame ass friends were the same way! And you, Ms. Goodie-Two-Shoes, made me the sickest of them all! No one is that sweet, nice, and polite! No one allows another person to make them feel less than nothing, and then act like nothing ever happened the next day! I watched Amanda all but spit on you, and you still never stood up for yourself! Ugh! Fuck normal! Because if that's normal, then I'll choose to be insane any day!"

CHAPTER THIRTY-TWO

"But what about Ray?" I ask, allowing the blood to trickle from my nose onto my jeans. I continue to antagonize her, "What about Ray's life? Did everyone's life sicken you but Ray's?"

She looks at her brother lovingly, "Ray has always taken good care of me. Even when everyone else in the house would gang up on me, Ray always had my back. It was like, everyone's favorite girl was always Amanda. Amanda was the pretty one, Amanda got better grades, Amanda, Amanda, Amanda, but not Ray. Ray always treated me like I was his favorite." She smiles at the thought until it fades suddenly.

"But Ray left for school, even though I begged him to stay. He left me in a house where no one understood me. Then you came along, and I thought, 'Maybe you could replace Ray,' you know? 'Maybe you would make me your favorite person.' Unfortunately, that wasn't the case. You never once thought to try to be a sister to me, only Amanda. So, there I was, in a house with a bunch of people that hated me. The only person in the world that ever loved me left. It was too much to bear at times." Her eyes fill with tears once she starts feeling sorry for herself. She wipes them away quickly.

"So, just like always, after I took matters into my own hands, big brother showed up to save the day. Thank God he went to school for psychotherapy! He advised me to act

completely fucking crazy so that my sanity plea would
stick. He even gave me heads up on the questions the
psychiatrists were going to ask so I could practice
producing the most outlandish answers. Even though they
deemed me competent at the time of the murders and
sentenced me to death, I was eventually sent to the mental
hospital after my ability to respond to regular commands
drastically declined. I played the role of 'crazy' so well,
they didn't think I could walk anymore. They figured I'd
completely popped my top after realizing what I did and
imploded because of it. I was ecstatic to find out that Kane
psych ward was a limited security hospital. It gave me the
motivation I needed to keep up this crazy charade for five
years. Now, most of my days are spent unsupervised.
According to my chart, I'm 'barely responsive', and in a
'vegetable-like state'. So, I usually roam around as often as
I want. That's how I found out about this place." I make a
slightly disturbed, but impressed face. I turn my attention to
Ray.

"You were just willing to go along with this, then?
Jeopardize everything you've worked so hard to
accomplish?" He looks embarrassed by the line of
questioning.

"I mean, Lizzie is my sister, and if I don't protect
her, then who will?"

"But she killed your other sister! Amanda…
remember her?" Liz slaps me again without warning,
gashing my lip this time. I spit the swiftly accumulating
blood from my mouth onto the floor near my feet.

"Fuck Amanda! She wasn't our sister; she was your
sister!" Ray looks as if he disagrees, even though he
doesn't vocalize it. I try to make eye contact with him, but
he ignores my obvious glares.

"Bro, what time is it?" Liz asks randomly.

"A little after eight," he answers after glancing at his watch, "Why? Are you about to head back to the hospital?"

"Yeah," she responds, walking towards the bathroom. Ray lets out a sigh of relief after she closes the door.

"Ray, you know this whole situation is crazy, right?" I point out in a low voice. Ray finally engages with me after trying his best not to do so.

"I do, but Lizzie has always been… special." He makes a face as if he pulled the word, "special", from the clear, blue sky. I smack my lips at his efforts to downplay the situation.

"Ray, you two have literally conspired to set me up for a crime I didn't commit! That's not special, that's cruel and flat out wrong!" He looks away from me like he secretly agrees. Liz comes out of the bathroom wearing a nurse's outfit. "Nurse Maggie" is displayed neatly on her name tag. I narrow my eyes at her.

I can't believe I didn't recognize her sooner!

"Ray, I've been thinking. We didn't think this plan through thoroughly. What are we going to do after the tape of her confession makes it to the police? Even if you keep her doped up until the authorities pick her up, once she gets a chance to sober up, she's going to sing like a canary bird. We can't chance it." Ray gawks at her as if she's getting on his nerves.

"Lizzie, telling her the truth was your idea! If we would've left it at what I convinced her to be the truth, you would've been home free! I'm the one that got her to believe she committed the murders, remember?" Liz rubs his back like she's trying to calm him down.

"I know, big brother, and that was my bad, but I've thought of a solution to fix that." We both stare at her while waiting for her to finish. She grins before continuing. "We kill her." My eyes get big at her declaration. So does Ray's.

"Kill her?" Ray asks as if he didn't hear her the first time. She nods her head yes, "Lizzie, I never agreed to any of that. I said I would help you get out, not kill Britney!" He gets upset with his words. She bends down to look in his eyes.

"This will help me get out, Ray." He looks at her as if he doesn't believe her, "Ray, you literally transferred to that hospital just so we could execute my plan properly. Don't tell me you want to quit now." Ray allows his sister to talk him into yet another awful idea. He finally nods his head in agreement. "Good," she says sweetly before kissing him on the cheek. She stands up to address me next.

"Sorry, Brit, but you're the one that wanted to know the truth. Unfortunately, that info cost you the ultimate price. Now I know why your life was spared that night; It was spared for the purpose of saving me from being executed. I won't be seeing you again; I gotta get back to the hospital and into my room before the orderlies notice I'm gone. I just wanted you to know that this is really great, what you're doing for me and all. You turned out to be a good sister after all."

CHAPTER THIRTY-THREE

An evil smile appears on Liz's face before she walks towards the basement door. She disappears down the stairs, and eventually, through the corridor leading to the hospital. I try to reason with Ray as soon as the coast is clear.

"You know she did that on purpose, right?" I ask, watching Ray get up from his seat and put it back in its spot at the dining room table.

"Did what?" He responds in an uninterested tone.

"Told me what was really going on here. She just needed a reason to convince you to kill me. She wants me dead. She's wanted me dead since that night she killed Amanda!" Ray acts as if he's ignoring me, even though I know he's not. I desperately keep talking, "She said it herself; she hates me most of all. She hates me because I'm a good person, something she could never be!"

"Shut up, Britney! You have no idea what the fuck you're talking about! My sister is a good person-"

"I can tell by the way she murdered five people!" Ray rushes towards me after interrupting him like he wants to paint my face with more blood. I stare at him with serious, teary eyes. He calms down slightly once he connects with them. He kneels in front of me like he usually does.

"She's my sister, Brit. She's the only one I have left. I have to protect her."

"So, you're going to just kill me, then?" I cry out as if I don't understand, "I know you think you were faking with our relationship, but I don't think you were. I think you really do care about me, Ray. I think you really do love me." He stands up suddenly as if my outcry of emotion is bothering him. He moves towards his duffle bag but puts his head down as soon as he reaches it.

"Of course I love you," he says so low, I can barely hear him. A small amount of hope radiates through me.

"I love you, too, Ray." He spins around to look at me.

"But I love my sister, too." I become devastated after realizing there's nothing I can say to change his mind. He walks towards the kitchen sink.

The noise of the knife being removed from its holder catches my ear. My heart rate speeds up once my eyes catch the sparkle of the huge blade. He stares at it with nervous eyes, and then at me. He holds it down to his side while he slowly moves in my direction.

"Ray! Please don't! This isn't you!" I shout, wriggling in my chair like I'm trying to get free. The dangerous point of the sharp metal object looks scarier the closer it gets to me.

"I'm so sorry, Brit," he mumbles with a shaky voice. Tears rush down his face, revealing how upset this whole situation is making him, too. My belly hurts violently when the knife gets within inches of me. I hurl almost instantly, leaning to the side and relieving myself on the living room floor.

"Please, don't," I manage to say again after expelling all my stomach contents near my feet. Ray jumps back from the splashing liquid with a look of disgust on his face.

"What's been going on with you? I've never known you to be this sickly."

"You would be, too, if the only man you've ever loved is threatening to kill you." Ray shakes his head as if that's not what he means.

"No. Think about it, Brit. You've been throwing up for days now. You'd have no appetite, and then eat everything in sight. You've been sleeping like crazy, too-"

"That's the medicine, I thought," I add quickly. Ray sighs before lifting my chin up to look into his eyes.

"When was your last period?" The question catches me off guard. I try to think back but realize I'm having a hard time remembering much of anything before we moved here.

"I- I don't know." Ray stares at me seriously for a few seconds before walking around to the back of my chair. He cuts the rope holding me in place. It falls to the floor after a few moments. I display a confused expression.

"Go and get it."

"Get what?" I ask, standing up slowly from the hard chair.

"The pregnancy test. I saw it in your top drawer."

***

"I still don't remember buying this thing," I admit, while waiting for the results to pop up on the white stick. I stare at Ray's nervous face through the bathroom mirror.

"I do. You bought it while we were staying in Amanda's old apartment in Atlanta. You kept mentioning that we were going to start a family soon." My eyes grow round with shock.

"Wait a minute, so we really did live there? I knew it!" I exclaim as if I get some sort of prize for being right. Ray turns his body towards mine.

"Yes, you were right about everything. The plan that Lizzie created was going to take a lot of time, effort, and patience. After transferring to Kane Hospital, I had to come up with an elaborate story about my past, create fake files and newspaper articles about the murders, act like a patient, and wait for us to cross paths in hopes that you didn't recognize me."

"That's insane," I say with a head shake. Ray sighs after my words.

"I can't say that I disagree."

"What about the video you showed me? The one I looked horrible in? I definitely resembled a mental patient."

"That was a mixture of drugs and hypnosis. I first started drugging you when you began visiting me in the rec room at the hospital a couple years ago. I knew that certain meds needed to be in your system for a long period of time before they started to work. That's partly how I got you to forget your past. That, and a little hypnotherapy once you passed out. The meds were cruel, so I had to take you into my office as soon as they took effect. I'd let you rest there. Then, when you were coming out of it, I'd tie you to a chair and record you. You were only saying the things we were talking about right before you passed out; You, me, our relationship… things like that."

I frown up at his confession. I can't believe the lengths he's been going through to please his sister. Ray is just as crazy as she is.

I must find a way to get far away from them both!

"It's time," Ray blurts out, staring at his watch. He takes a deep breath before looking at me. I swallow hard while reaching for the test. I compare it to the pictures on the box.

"So… What does it say?" Ray asks impatiently. My stares go from the stick to his eyes.

"It's two pink lines. That means I'm pregnant." A feeling of disbelief comes over me. I gawk at the stick, hoping that the second line will disappear at any second. I become obsessed with my wish until Ray breaks the silence.

"You are?" He asks in an almost happy tone. I look taken aback by his reaction.

"Why do you sound like this is good news?" I inquire angrily.

Being pregnant is the last thing I want to be in a situation like this!

"Because it sort of is." I take a perplexed step away from him.

"Ray, you were just about to kill me a few minutes ago! You do realize that, right? If I never would've thrown up at the last minute, you would've killed me and this baby with no problem!" Ray grabs me and kisses me without warning. I forcefully shove him away from me.

"What the fuck is wrong with you! You think I want to be with you after all of this? You're just as crazy as your sister is!" Ray takes a few unfazed steps towards the hallway.

"One second," he says before disappearing from my sight. I follow behind him cautiously. He takes a sheet of paper from his duffle bag, "Here."

I hesitate before removing it from his hand. I open it up to read what it says.

"Marriage License?" I blurt out in a confused tone. My eyes jump to the signatures at the bottom, "This paper says that we're married." I look at Ray for validation. He nods his head to confirm it's true. I shake my head in disbelief, "What?"

"We really did get married, baby. You really are my wife."

CHAPTER THIRTY-FOUR

"I- I don't understand," I admit while staring at the document. Ray steps backwards towards the couch and sits on it.

"We really did get married six months ago." I glare at him silently as I try to make sense of what he's saying.

"Why? Why marry me when the only reason we were together in the first place was so that you can set me up?" Ray sighs as if the question is a difficult one. He looks ashamed before turning away from my piercing stare.

"I think it's time for me to tell you the truth. The real truth. The entire truth."

Even though I'm interested in what he's saying, I still keep my distance. I gawk at him while waiting for him to continue.

"When my sister talked me into doing this for her, I knew it was wrong. The only thing that made me go along with it was my love for her. Like I said, she was the only sister I had left, and I don't know, I guess I kind of felt like her killing Amanda was my fault. If I would've never left home, she never would've done what she did." I shake my head as if I disagree. He ignores me.

"I knew you were my adopted sister, but I never built a relationship with you. You were an eleven-year-old girl and I was going to college, so we literally had nothing in common; And since I moved out the year you got there, I hardly laid eyes on you. Every time I came home, you looked like a totally different person. You were growing up. I guess I was never around enough to care. That's why it was so easy for me to agree to this crazy ass plan. My rationale, as dumb as it sounds, was that I didn't know much about you anyway, so it was no big deal for you to take the fall for my sister. Lizzie was my blood, but you weren't." I fold my arms as if I'm offended by what I'm hearing. He hesitantly continues.

"When I first saw you after all of those years, I was floored. I mean, you were gorgeous! You had me speechless! I tried to dismiss my attraction to you, but it was too strong to ignore. Even so, I still tried to go along with my sister's plan." He finally looks me in my eyes, "Originally, I was supposed to pump you full of drugs and fuck with your mind. I would rewrite your memories with hypnosis, and then force you to confess to a crime you didn't commit-"

"Which is what you did," I blurt out in an unpleasant tone. He disagrees instantly.

"No. I was supposed to get that done in six months tops, but the more I got to know you, the more I felt like I couldn't do it."

"Why not?"

"Because I fell in love with you, Brit. I needed you. You made me feel so comfortable, and you made me feel important. You treated me like I deserved the world, even though you thought I committed those terrible ass crimes. I've never met someone with a heart as beautiful as yours." I'm flattered by his words, even though I'm trying my hardest not to show it. He stands up to continue his story.

"So, as you could guess, I was in one hell of a predicament. All Lizzie talked about was being a free woman, so I couldn't exactly tell her that I was having a change of heart. She would've taken it upon herself to finish out the plan on her own, and believe me, that would've been the worst possible thing to happen. She's sloppy, impulsive, and dangerous when her fragile mind isn't balanced. If she didn't kill you, then you would have wished you were dead."

His words send fearful chills down my spine. He steps closer to me like he wants to wrap his arms around me but doesn't. Things start to get awkward between us, so he starts talking again.

"I had to pick a side, and I had to pick it quickly. On one hand, I had my sister that I've taken care of since she was born. As unstable as she is, I still adored her. I made being there for her my duty, especially since no one else in the family seemed to be interested in doing so. We all deserve unconditional love, even the ones that are rough around the edges."

He looks at me with loving eyes, "And on the other hand, there was you. Even though you've been in my life for over a decade, I still didn't know you. It wasn't until you started walking in that rec room to visit me that I realized I couldn't live without you. You heard all of those awful things about me, but they never shook your stance; I was the man of your dreams, and I was going to be your husband. I felt the same way about you being my wife." Tears gather in my eyes as his sincere words make my heart flutter. He finally touches me softly on the hips.

"I chose you, baby. I chose you. My sister's life is over, but mine isn't, so I think it's about time I start living it for me, and not for her anymore."

***

"There's still a few things I don't understand," I admit while throwing a few of my items in my suitcase. Ray pulls out his luggage and starts packing up a few of his items as well.

"Only a few?" He asks jokingly, even though the situation is a heavy one. I nod my head yes.

"Things like, why am I still having a hard time remembering my past?"

"Because, you still have some drugs in your system." I stop what I'm doing after remembering him feeding me an unknown pill last night. I turn to look at him.

"If you chose me, then why was I still taking medication?"

"Because your doses were so high before that I had to wean you off of it. Right before we got married, I started administering you smaller milligrams and did so until you got down to a dose safe enough to take you off completely."

"So, I don't take psych meds anymore?" I ask in a confused tone.

"Nope," he answers quickly.

"Well, what did I take last night, then?" Ray reaches in his pocket and pulls out the bag holding the pills. He stares at them, and then at me.

"Prenatal vitamins." I gawk at him with perplexed eyes. I take the bag from his hand.

"Prenatal vitamins?"

"Yup. I kind of figured you were pregnant. I found some at the hospital; and I was the one that really bought the pregnancy test, not you." I glance at him after studying the pills.

"How did you know?"

"I've been trying to get you pregnant since I stopped giving you those psych drugs a couple months ago. I had the test and the prenatal vitamins on standby just in case we needed them. I'm surprised I knocked you up this quickly. I thought I was shooting blanks all of these years."

"Apparently not," I say, looking down at my midsection that's now home to our small bundle of joy. Ray sticks his hand out slowly.

"May I?" He asks. I nod my head yes. He lays his hand on my abdomen, "I can't believe you're carrying around a part of me inside of you."

I look around at the crazy situation we're in, "Me, neither."

CHAPTER THIRTY-FIVE

After packing up as much stuff as we can, Ray drags both of our suitcases to the front door. He sighs before turning around to face me.

"I'm so sorry, baby... For everything. You didn't deserve to go through any of this." He kisses me on the cheek before reaching for the doorknob, but I stop him.

"If you decided not to go through with her plan before we even came here, then why did we? Why did you put me through all this torture, convince me that I'm a maniac, and then record me saying those terrible things if you never intended for your sister and I to switch fates in the first place?"

"A couple of reasons. First of all, if we never would've showed up, my sister would've came looking for us. As you can see, she leaves the hospital whenever she pleases, so it would be nothing for her to find her way into the city."

"I still don't get how she's able to roam around so freely without being detected."

"The same way I was able to play a doctor and a patient. That place is horrible. It's terribly kept and extremely understaffed. Those workers don't give a damn about anything that goes on there. They don't even do their rounds like they're supposed to do." I shake my head in disbelief, " Second of all, I never recorded you saying anything, but I have been recording Lizzie." My eyes get big with his confession.

"Wait a minute, are you saying-"

"Yes. I really came here to get proof that she's not in the bedridden state they think she's in. My sister is a danger to society. I see that now. She doesn't need to be moving about freely, she needs to be locked up in a high security prison. I still went through certain parts of the plan to buy me some time. She was always watching us, just like she's watching us now." Ray stares at the basement doorway while putting his truck keys in my hand.

"Get in the driver's seat. If I'm not out in two minutes, leave without me."

"No!" I shout, grabbing him by his arm. He looks at me seriously.

"You and my baby are the only people that's important right now. I need to make sure you're safe-"

"You heard our fake sister. She said no," Liz says from the darkness of the basement stairs. She slowly emerges, sporting her patient uniform instead of her Nurse Maggie costume. Ray slides me behind him slowly. He glares at his sister.

"I knew you were standing there," he mentions sternly. Liz holds a butcher knife in one hand and plays with its blade with the other.
"How did you know?" She asks, stepping closer to us. Ray eases us against the front door.

"Because, after I cut the ropes off of Britney, I set that knife on the kitchen table. Once I noticed it was missing, I kind of figured you were the one that took it." Liz pauses after his words.

"Why did you just say all of those things, then, if you knew I could hear you?"

"Because you needed to hear them." She looks taken aback, and then amused. She paces the floor in front of us.

"Wow, Ray. So, you were just going to abandon me like everyone else in our family did, huh?" Anger can be heard underneath her sarcastic tone. Ray's hand brushes against the doorknob.

"Lizzie, you need help. I love you, but I can't allow you to be free. Not now, not ever." She stops suddenly in her tracks as if his words paralyzed her. She stares at him with wet eyes.

"What happened to 'you and me against the world'? What happened to you taking care of me no matter what?" Ray twists the knob, causing the door to open slightly. Liz hears the door creak ajar as tears run down her cheeks. She makes a broken-hearted expression.

"You're a grown woman now, Elizabeth. I can't take care of you anymore. I have to be there for my wife and child." Liz's stares suddenly dart my way. Fire burns in her eyes almost instantly. She gawks at me sideways as if a sinister presence has taken over her body.

"You bitch! First, you take Amanda from me, and now my brother?! You fucking bitch!" Liz raises her knife and sprints towards me. Ray swings the door open quickly and pushes me out of it. His back catches the blade when he jumps in between me and his sister.

"Run!" He exclaims while trying his best not to buckle from the deep knife wound.

"No! Ray!" I scream before he closes the door and locks it. I run for the truck and jump inside. I pull out of the driveway wildly, hitting the curb before putting the car in drive. I speed down the makeshift street until it opens to a big area of concrete. I exit the hospital grounds, crying hysterically as Kane Mental Hospital shows prominently in the rear-view mirror.

***

"There! It's right there!" I yell while pointing to the house Ray and I were staying in. The police officer pulls in front of the home immediately.

"Stay here," he demands as he exits the car. The ambulance pulls up behind us with their emergency lights flashing just like the squad car I'm sitting in. I watch closely with anticipation as the cop pounds on the door.

"Police! Open up!" He gets no answer. He pounds once more, "I said, police! If you don't open this door, then I'm going to kick it down!" No one answers again, so he kicks at the door with a hard strike. The force nearly knocks it off its hinges.

"Medics!" The officer shouts after sticking his head inside. My heart beats rapidly as the suspense of the situation all but kills me. The EMTs rush inside the house to check on the scene. One comes out a few seconds later to retrieve the gurney.

"Fuck this," I mumble, jumping out of the car. I rush towards the house, but the cop stops me as soon as he sees me coming.

"No! No, you can't interfere with the crime scene!" My eyes go straight to Ray's body lying on the living room floor.

"Nooo! Nooo!" I scream while trying to get closer to my husband. The paramedics tend to his lifeless body in desperation.

"Please God, no! Ray!" I shout repeatedly, disappearing in a river of my own tears. I hit the ground after losing all the strength in my legs. The officer helps me to his car.

"Ma'am, didn't you mention to me that you're pregnant?" He asks after easing me back into my seat. I eventually nod my head yes.

"Well then, you need to calm down. Let the medics do their jobs." I catch a glimpse of Ray being rolled swiftly towards the ambulance. I visually search his body for any signs of life, but I'm unable to find any. One of the EMTs rushes over to us.

"He's alive, but barely. He has multiple stab wounds, and he's lost a lot of blood. He needs medical attention ASAP, so we're going to take him to Kane's since we're already here. The doctors should be able to help him there."

CHAPTER THIRTY-SIX

"You can't go back there with him," a nurse grabs me and says as the medical staff rapidly wheel Ray through a set of double doors. I face her, noticing her outfit is identical to the one Liz wears while playing Nurse Maggie, "Dr. Monroe is going straight in for emergency surgery. I'll report updates to you as soon as they become available." She gives me a caring grin before disappearing behind the swiftly moving doctors. I stand at the entrance, feeling completely shattered and hopeless.

"He's going to be fine," the police officer assures me from behind. I turn around slowly to face him.

"What about the person who did this, his sister, Elizabeth? Where is she?" I ask eagerly. He takes off his hat before addressing my concerns.

"My guys swept that entire strip of houses, but they didn't find her. They even checked that tunnel you told us about, but she wasn't there, either." I look around with fearful eyes. He places his hand on my shoulder.

"Hey, I'm almost sure she didn't come back here. I know if I were her, I'd try to escape this place. I'm sure one of my men will find her trying to bum a ride on the interstate or something."

"I don't know, sir. She claimed she's been roaming around this hospital freely for years, so if she wanted to leave, she would have done so by now."

The officer's radio goes off, startling us both. He reaches for it after hearing dispatch, "I have to take this." He turns around and walks towards the other end of the hallway. I look around for a women's bathroom after realizing I've been holding my pee for hours. I rush into a stall as soon as I bust through the restroom door. I relieve myself immediately.

I wipe my private area and pull my pants up. I try to fix its button but stop once I hear the door open. I freeze with unbelievable fear. I listen to the slow footsteps moving about the bathroom floor. I lean down to glance underneath my stall door. My eyes glaze over with terror once I spot the nurse shoes moving towards me. The pair of feet stop once they near the stall I'm in.

"Mrs. Monroe?" I hear, instantly recognizing the voice as the nurse from earlier. I let out a huge sigh of relief while unlocking and opening the stall door.

"How is he?" I inquire immediately, walking past her and towards the sink. I turn around and stare at her impatiently.

"He's fighting. He was stabbed twice in the back, and once in the chest. The knife did a lot of damage, but it missed all his vital organs. He has a high probability of making a full recovery." Relieved tears burst from my eyes. She smiles as if she's happy to give me some positive news.

"When can I see him?"

"Soon. He's being stitched up right now. I'll come and get you as soon as he's stable."

***

I open my eyes to an empty waiting room. Before I dozed off, there were half a dozen people sitting around me. Now, the receptionist behind the desk has even disappeared. I stand up from my seat to find the time.

"3:03 a.m.," I mumble after spotting a clock on the wall. I swallow hard at the sight of the familiar hour.

"Hello!" I shout once I approach the waiting room desk. I wait for a response, but there is none. "Hello!" I yell again, easing down the hallway this time. I know it's late, but there still should be some staff around here somewhere. I peer into random, empty rooms as I pass them.

Ray was right. This place is extremely understaffed.

I eventually make it to the double doors they rushed Ray through when we first arrived. The fear of walking through them paralyzes me.

What if something went wrong with Ray's surgery and that's the reason why the nurse never came back out to get me? What if Ray is dead?!

Tears gather in my eyes for the millionth time before trickling down my face. I place my hand against my womb when our baby crosses my mind. The thought of us being parents gives me the courage I need to keep going.

Ray is going to be around for the birth of our child, I just know he is!

I proceed cautiously through the doors, looking around carefully as soon as I cross the threshold. I let out a huge sigh of relief once I spot a nurse walking towards the other end of the hallway.

"Excuse me! Miss!" I shout out in her direction. She pauses once she hears my voice.

"Miss!" I shout again, jogging towards her this time. She remains still as I near her.

"Nurse? I was hoping you could help me. I'm looking for my husband. He was rushed back here for surgery a while ago, but no one has updated me on his status yet."

"Your husband is dead," she says in a cold tone. I gasp loudly at the sound of her evil voice. Liz turns around slowly to face me, "I should know, because I killed him."

CHAPTER THIRTY-SEVEN

Liz lunges towards me after her words, but I jump to the side instinctively. I run at record speed down the hallway until I hit a dead end.

"Shit!" I exclaim, looking around for escape options. I spot a door labeled "stairs" and rush towards it. Realizing that I'm already on the first floor, I sprint to the second floor. I waste no time bursting through the door with a huge "2" covering it.

"Help me!" I shout as soon as I exit the stairwell. The bloody corpses scattered throughout the hallway send shockwaves throughout my body.

"Oh… my… God," I mutter, covering my mouth to stop myself from throwing up. Orderlies and nurse's bodies litter my path. I step over them carefully while trying to get to the other end of the hallway.

"Hello?" I exclaim after slowly turning the corner. More hospital workers lay dead in the hallway. I cover my mouth again while I quickly pass them. I shriek when a security guard grabs my ankle.

"Please… Please, help me," he cries out in a pain-filled voice. I glance down at the blood oozing from the wounds on his chest.

"I'm going to bring back help," I say in a sympathetic tone. I break away from his grasp, deciding to desperately keep moving.

"Brit-ney..." I jump after hearing my name being spoken sarcastically over the hospital's loudspeakers. Liz giggles as if she knows she scared me, "I have a confession to make. I didn't really kill Ray. He is actually doing just fine. He's high on painkillers and under heavy sedation in room 228. Meet me there in five minutes, unless you want me to finish what I started. He chose you over me; Now, will you choose him over you?"

I stand in the middle of the bloody hallway, slowly processing the things she said. I glance at the room number I'm standing near:

"Room 210," I whisper to myself. I think hard about my next move...

Ray would want me to flee, especially for the sake of our child, but I can't just walk away and let her kill him. I wouldn't be able to live with myself.

"I'm going," I decide quickly. I walk inside room 210, trying my best not to agitate the patient that's strapped down to the bed. He stares at me with bucked eyes but maintains his silence. I start rummaging through the drawers' contents immediately.

"Bingo," I mutter when I find a scalpel. I slide it securely in my back pocket. I peek both ways down the hall before rejoining the gruesome scene.

After making sure I'm headed in the right direction, I take quiet steps towards room 228. I hesitate slightly once I approach it.

"This is it," I think after pausing to take a few deep breaths. I glance around the room's corner, trying my best not to make my presence known yet. My eyes instantly land on Liz standing next to Ray's bandaged body. So much blood is smeared on the front of her nursing uniform, you'd think she was wounded, too. She strokes Ray's arm gently.

"You know, when I was a little girl, Ray would come in my room every night to tuck me in. He would tell me a story or talk to me about his day. It didn't matter what he said to me, honestly, as long as I got to see his face before I went to sleep."

Liz starts talking to me, letting me know that she knows I'm standing outside the door. I ease in slowly as she wipes the tears from her eyes. She doesn't bother looking up at me.

"I remember staring into his light-colored eyes in amazement. Since no one else in the family had eyes like his, I thought he was an alien, superhero, or something." She giggles at the memory, but her smile fades once her eyes finally meet mine.

"It wasn't until I saw momma's co-worker when we were at the grocery store one day that I realized that Ray had eyes just like him. Turns out, I wasn't the only one that noticed. That was the first time I ever saw daddy hit momma. Unfortunately, it wasn't the last."

She sighs at the painful memory, "That's why I never understood why they brought you home that day. I mean, wasn't our family complicated enough? Didn't we have enough problems?" She stares at me as if she still doesn't know the answers to those questions. She leans down and kisses Ray on the forehead softly. I catch a glimpse of the bloody knife laying on Ray's cover, causing me to swallow hard. We watch each other closely.

"That was quite a mess you made out there," I exclaim, referring to the hospital staff's bodies sprawled all over the hallway floors. She barely reacts to my words, but eventually humps her shoulders.

"I honestly wanted someone to stop me, but they were all so pathetic. This hospital has 16 people covering the night shift, including security. What a joke." She shakes her head after her words. I keep my eyes on her knife, "I just kept calling them to this floor using the hand radio, one by one. Not one of them put up a fight, not even the men. Can you believe that?" Liz finally picks up her weapon of choice and I take a nervous step back. She stares at me with a weird glare.

"What about you, Britney? Are you going to put up a fight?"

"You do know I'm pregnant, right?" I ask in a shaky voice. She nods her head as a response.

"I think I heard Ray say something about a wife and kid. Aww. You're on a roll, I see. First, you were his sister, then his wife, now his baby's mother. Are you auditioning to be his mom next?" My stomach turns at her inappropriate joke. She takes a step away from Ray's side and in my direction. I pull the scalpel from my pocket and hold it out in front of me. She chuckles at my attempt to defend myself.

"Well, at least that's better than what the others did. The security guard didn't even draw his gun." She shakes her head disappointedly.

"You're just going to kill the woman carrying your niece or nephew?" Liz places her hands on her hips with an offended expression.

"Are you seriously trying to use family ties as a reasoning tactic with a woman that has killed and seriously wounded two of her own family members?" The panic sets in after I realize I'm not going to be able to talk her out of this. She uses the silent moment to swing her knife at me. I jump back, but not far enough. She catches my shoulder with the tip of the blade. I howl out in pain once the sharp metal slices my skin open.

"That's it! Run!" She shrieks after I dart out of the room door. The blood squirting from the nasty cut leaks down my arm. I jog through the hallway while applying pressure to it. I rack my brain for survival options, but the extreme nature of the situation won't allow me to think straight.

"I'm going to catch you!" Liz yells in a kiddy tone. I turn around and notice she's chasing me. I try to run faster.

"No!" I scream after slipping in a pool of blood. I fall to the floor awkwardly. Liz stops moving once a wave of laughter crashes over her.

"Sorry, Brit, but you're as pathetic as the rest of these losers!" She spits out between chuckles. I try to stand, but the newfound pain in my ankle stops me from doing so. A feeling of defeat engulfs me. Frightened tears run down my face once she starts coming towards me again. She wipes the knife's blade across the front of her clothes, "Let's get this over with, shall we?"

CHAPTER THIRTY-EIGHT

I look around frantically for something to defend myself with. I spot the scalpel I was toting a few feet in front of me, but quickly decide it's too far away for me to try and reach it. I glance around desperately again.

"The security guard!" I think once I spot his body lying behind me. He appears to be dead now, but his gun is still on his waist, just like Liz said. I slide over to him quickly, unbutton his holster, and clumsily snatch his gun from his hip. I rapidly point it at an approaching Liz. She pauses with a look of surprise.

"Do you even know how to use that thing?" She asks in a mocking tone. The gun shakes noticeably in my trembling hands.

"I know that all I have to do is pull this little lever to blow your crazy ass away!" Liz nods her head at my statement.

"That's good and all, but won't you have to remove the safety, first?" I make a bewildered expression before staring at the gun. She rushes towards me, prompting me to squeeze the trigger.

It won't budge.

My eyes grow wide when she draws the bloody knife back. She swings it wildly at my neck, striking it with so much force, my head nearly-

"Mrs. Monroe? Mrs. Monroe, we have news about your husband." I scream out of my sleep, grabbing my neck tightly with both hands. Tears run down my terrified face. The nurse looks startled by my actions, prompting her to bend down to tend to me. "Hey, are you OK?"

"Liz… she- she was here… she tried to kill me!" I stutter through heavy breaths. The lady sits down before wrapping her arm around me.

"Oh, no. Liz isn't here, the police picked her up hours ago. The chief asked if I could relay the message to you since he had to go. They have her in custody now."

A relieved look covers my face. "And my husband?" I ask in a hopeful tone.

"He's doing well. He's out of surgery, and now he's asking for you." I stand to my feet quickly.

"So, when can I see him?" She stands up, too.

"Right now. Follow me."

***

"Ray?" I say softly as I touch his arm. He opens his eyes and looks at me.

"Britney?" I smile at the sound of his voice.

"Yes, it's me."

"Thank God," he says, grabbing my hand with his. "Where's-"

"The police found her. She's in custody," I answer before he gets the question out. He lets out the same sigh of relief I did when I found out.

"It's over," he says emotionally. I kiss him on the forehead.

"Yes, it's finally over. Now, our family will be safe."

***

ONE YEAR LATER

I place Ray Jr.'s little body inside of his crib after rocking him to sleep. I click on his nightlight before easing out of his room. I find my husband sitting on the edge of our bed. I walk in our room to join him.

"He's asleep already?" He asks without looking up at me. I flop down next to him.

"Yup. He was exhausted today. I guess all of that fussing earlier tired him out." Ray finally takes his eyes off the papers in his hands. He leans over and kisses me sweetly. He sits the paperwork on the bed before he stands up to go inside of our walk-in closet. I glance at the documents.

"So, what is the board saying?"

"That my license is still suspended," he answers from a distance. I make a troubled face.

"Well, how are you feeling about that?" He walks out the closet wearing flannel pajama pants and no shirt. I bite my lip at the sight of his chiseled chest.

"Grateful. They can suspend my medical license indefinitely for all I care. As long as I don't have to go to prison."

I nod my head as if I understand, especially since he was already arrested for his involvement in his sister's plan right after he got out of the hospital. Surprisingly, Liz went on record saying that she made him participate, and that the only reason he went along with it was because she threatened to kill me if he didn't. They released Ray right after that. Unfortunately, he had already missed five months of my pregnancy.

He moves the paperwork from the bed to the dresser. He turns around slowly, gesturing for me to lay down. I happily do what he says. He crawls on top of me shortly thereafter.

"You ready for another baby?" He asks while staring in my eyes. I blush at the offer, but shake my head no.

"I think we should wait until I don't have to work anymore. Being pregnant with Ray Jr. made my job 10 times harder." He nods his head like he understands, even though a look of disappointment covers his face. He rolls off me.

"I'm sorry that I'm putting you through this, baby. I've always dreamed of being a graphic designer, but I had no idea that the starting pay would be so lousy!"

"Compared to being a doctor, I'm sure any other job's starting pay would be considered lousy." I smile after my words, but he doesn't find my statement humorous. I roll over and lay on top of him.

"Ray, everything is going to be OK. We'll figure everything out."

"But what if I never get my license back?"

"Then we'll leave the medical field in the rearview mirror. You're capable of much more than that, anyway." I softly kiss his lips after my words, "And just because we're not having another baby right this second doesn't mean we can't practice."

Ray wraps his arms around me tightly once we fall into a deep make-out session. We roll our bodies around the king- sized bed with him ending up on top of me. Things are heated between us when his cell phone rings. He kisses me a few more times before checking the caller I.D. His eyes react strangely to what he reads.

"It's the police department."

"The police department?" I ask quickly. He nods his head yes. He climbs off me before answering.

"Hello?... Yes, this is he... I'm sorry, what?... What do you mean they're dead?! That's impossible, I just talked to them!... No, I will not calm down!... What?!... And why wasn't I notified!"

Ray continues yelling at the top of his lungs, waking Ray Jr. from his slumber. I rush to him after hearing his cries.

"It's OK, baby. It's OK," I say in a soothing voice. He stares at me with his bright hazel eyes before I pick him up and place him against my chest.

"Britney!" Ray shouts, startling the baby once more. I pat his back when he begins crying again. I hurry back to our bedroom with Ray Jr. securely in my arms. I stare at my husband, waiting for him to divulge the information that has him so up in arms.

"They're dead!" He shouts, pacing the floor quickly. Tears stream down his distraught face.

"Who's dead, honey?" I ask in a worried voice.

"Mom and dad! Mom and dad are dead!" My jaw hits the floor.

"What! How?" I exclaim, upsetting Ray Jr. even more. He cries loudly, but I'm in too much shock to calm him down.

"They were stabbed," Ray answers in an eerie tone. He looks at me with a terrified glare.

"No!" I shout, letting the news knock tears from my eyes. Chill bumps form on every inch of my skin.

"Lizzie escaped last night. They haven't been able to locate her. They think she killed our parents, and now, they believe she's on her way here to do the same thing to us."